Getting Even

Getting Even
Gripping Tales of Revenge

Compiled by
Diana King

THE BOBBS-MERRILL COMPANY, INC.
Indianapolis/New York

Library of Congress Cataloging in Publication Data
Main entry under title:
Getting even.
    1. Short stories, American.   2. Short stories,
English.   3. Revenge—Fiction.   I. King, Diana.
PZ1.G3198   [PS648.R48]   823'.01   77-15441
ISBN 0-672-52397-3

*This anthology is dedicated to
my son, Butch*

Acknowledgments

"Sredni Vashtar" by Saki (H. H. Munro), copyright © 1930, 1958 by The Viking Press, Inc. From *The Complete Short Stories of Saki* (H. H. Munro). All rights reserved. Reprinted by permission of The Viking Press.

"The Chink and the Child" by Thomas Burke. From *Limehouse Nights*, copyright 1917 by Robert M. McBride Co., Inc. Permission to use this story is granted by John Farquharson Ltd. on behalf of the Estate of Thomas Burke.

"Wash" by William Faulkner, copyright 1934 and renewed 1962 by William Faulkner. Reprinted from *Collected Stories of William Faulkner*, by permission of Random House, Inc.

"Mary Postgate" by Rudyard Kipling, copyright 1915 by Rudyard Kipling from *A Diversity of Creatures* by Rudyard Kipling. Reprinted by permission of Doubleday & Company, Inc. and the Executors of the Estate of Mrs. George Bambridge.

"A Duel by Candlelight" by Andreas Latzko. Reprinted by permission of Esquire Magazine; © 1936 by Esquire, Inc.

"Roman Fever" by Edith Wharton. Reprinted with the permission of Charles Scribner's Sons from *The Collected Short Stories of Edith Wharton* by Edith Wharton. Copyright 1934 by Liberty Magazine.

Contents

Introduction
Diana King   xi

1 **Sredni Vashtar**
   Saki (H. H. Munro)   1

2 **The Chink and the Child**
   Thomas Burke   7

3 **Wash**
   William Faulkner   21

4 **Mary Postgate**
   Rudyard Kipling   37

5 **The Wolf**
   Guy de Maupassant   55

6 **A Duel by Candlelight**
   Andreas Latzko   62

7 **Roman Fever**
   Edith Wharton   76

8 **And Don't Forget the One Red Rose**
   Avram Davidson   93

9 **The Men Who Murdered Mohammed**
   Alfred Bester   100

10 **The Animal Fair**
   Robert Bloch   116

11 **The Jar**
   Ray Bradbury   132

12 **A Lot on His Mind**
   Bill Pronzini   150

13 **The Man on the Ground**
   Robert E. Howard   158

14 **The Kill**
   Peter Fleming   165

15 **Serenade for Baboons**
   Noel Langley   180

16 **Come Dance with Me on My Pony's Grave**
   C. L. Grant   193

Introduction

S. I. Hayakawa, that analyst of language in all its myriad uses, has observed that a reader identifies with the character in a story in two ways: first, he may see himself, or his own experience, as similar to that of the character; and second, he may see the character as dissimilar but identify with him anyway, because the character is fulfilling a desire that the reader has harbored but has never been able to attain in his own everyday existence.

Revenge stories seem to engage the reader in both ways. Everyone has at one time or another felt the desire to get even for some real or imagined transgression, but most of us never do it except in our fantasies. Thus we can easily identify with a revenge motivation and vicariously satisfy our own vengeful feelings by reading about someone else's getting even.

Perhaps for this reason literature is replete with works based on the theme of revenge. *Moby Dick* is a prime example. Clearly, Melville understood the need for getting even, and readers have identified strongly with Ahab's desire for revenge upon the whale (or God, nature, fate—

Melville says that Ahab "piled upon the whale's white hump the sum of all the general rage and hate felt by his whole race, from Adam down . . ."). Never one to think small, Ahab tells Starbuck, "I'd smite the sun if it insulted me"; and, extreme though his need for vengeance may be, readers have not only understood it but applauded it.

There are numerous other examples: *Othello* can easily be read as the story of Iago's revenge upon the Moor. *The Visit*, Friedrich Dürrenmatt's play, reveals the lengths to which a woman will go in order to get even with a man who has done her wrong. Carson McCullers's *Ballad of the Sad Café* is the story of Marvin Macy's revenge upon Amelia. And further back, there is the story of God's revenge upon the Egyptians, and upon His chosen people when they forsook Him; Circe's revenge upon Ulysses and his men; the gods' revenge upon Prometheus for delivering fire into the hands of men . . . the list could go on and on. Revenge stories have been popular almost since the beginning of literature itself.

The short stories in this book are a representative and entertaining sampling of what seem to be two major approaches to the theme of revenge: There is the realistic or direct approach, in which the main character takes it upon himself to exact vengeance with the tools at hand. Faulkner's "Wash," Kipling's "Mary Postgate," de Maupassant's "The Wolf," Latzko's "A Duel by Candlelight," Wharton's "Roman Fever," and Thomas Burke's "The Chink and the Child" are realistic stories in the sense that the characters take care of the matter themselves in a way that the reader can accept with very little "suspension of disbelief" on his part. The other approach involves a supernatural element: In Peter Fleming's "The Kill," it is a werewolf. C. L. Grant in "Come Dance with Me on My Pony's Grave" and Noel Langley in "Serenade for Baboons" explore the use of magic for vengeance. The revenge ghost so popular in Victorian literature appears briefly in Robert E. Howard's "The Man on the Ground" and is given a new twist in Bill Pronzini's "A Lot on His Mind."

The other stories are a mixture of everyday, familiar characters in bizarre, *outré* circumstances which give them an almost supernatural quality. The master of this kind of story is Saki, and "Sredni Vashtar" has the chilling aura of a supernatural tale without benefit of ghosts, werewolves, vampires or any of the numerous other "things that go bump in the night." Robert Bloch, Ray Bradbury, and Avram Davidson have also contributed stories that combine the mundane and the otherworldly to spine-tingling effect. And Alfred Bester in "The Men Who Murdered Mohammed" describes a "mad professor" who uses science to get even.

Regardless of the approach used by the writers, it's likely that their characters would agree with Confucius on the subject of revenge. When asked what he thought of using excellence to repay those who hate you, he said, "How then will you repay excellence? Do what is called for to repay those who hate you, and be excellent in return for excellence."

The creatures of the darkness that so often people the pages of horror stories (and the individual subconscious) equally often have revenge as their *raison d'être*. At the bottom of it all, perhaps, is fear—and knowledge on the gut level that, as Auden put it in "September 1, 1939":

> Accurate scholarship can
> Unearth the whole offence
> From Luther until now
> That has driven a culture mad,
> Find what occurred at Linz,
> What huge imago made
> A psychopathic god:
> I and the public know

Introduction

> What all schoolchildren learn,
> Those to whom evil is done
> Do evil in return.

If we're not the ones who are getting even, it's horrifyingly possible that we're the ones who will be gotten even with . . . in this world or the next. On the subject of evil, there seem to be few neutral corners in which to stand.

Diana King
New York City, 1978

Sredni Vashtar
by Saki (H. H. Munro)

Conradin was ten years old, and the doctor had pronounced
his professional opinion that the boy would not live another
five years. The doctor was silky and effete, and counted for
little, but his opinion was endorsed by Mrs. De Ropp, who
counted for nearly everything. Mrs. De Ropp was Conradin's
cousin and guardian, and in his eyes she represented those
three-fifths of the world that are necessary and disagreeable
and real; the other two-fifths, in perpetual antagonism to the
foregoing, were summed up in himself and his imagination.
One of these days Conradin supposed he would succumb to
the mastering pressure of wearisome necessary things—
such as illnesses and coddling restrictions and drawn-out
dullness. Without his imagination, which was rampant
under the spur of loneliness, he would have succumbed long
ago.

Mrs. De Ropp would never, in her honestest moments,
have confessed to herself that she disliked Conradin, though
she might have been dimly aware that thwarting him "for his
good" was a duty which she did not find particularly irk-
some. Conradin hated her with a desperate sincerity which

he was perfectly able to mask. Such few pleasures as he could contrive for himself gained an added relish from the likelihood that they would be displeasing to his guardian, and from the realm of his imagination she was locked out—an unclean thing which should find no entrance.

In the dull, cheerless garden, overlooked by so many windows that were ready to open with a message not to do this or that, or a reminder that medicines were due, he found little attraction. The few fruit-trees that it contained were set jealously apart from his plucking, as though they were rare specimens of their kind, blooming in an arid waste; it would probably have been difficult to find a market-gardener who would have offered ten shillings for their entire yearly produce. In a forgotten corner, however, almost hidden behind a dismal shrubbery, was a disused tool-shed of respectable proportions, and within its walls Conradin found a haven, something that took on the varying aspects of a playroom and a cathedral. He had peopled it with a legion of familiar phantoms, evoked partly from fragments of history and partly from his own brain, but it also boasted two inmates of flesh and blood. In one corner lived a ragged-plumaged Houdan hen, on which the boy lavished an affection that had scarcely another outlet. Further back in the gloom stood a large hutch, divided into two compartments, one of which was fronted with close iron bars. This was the abode of a large polecat-ferret which a friendly butcher-boy had once smuggled, cage and all, into its present quarters, in exchange for a long-secreted hoard of small silver. Conradin was dreadfully afraid of the lithe, sharp-fanged beast, but it was his most treasured possession. Its very presence in the tool-shed was a secret and fearful joy, to be kept scrupulously from the knowledge of the Woman, as he privately dubbed his cousin. And one day, out of Heaven knows what material, he spun the beast a wonderful name, and from that moment it grew into a god and a religion. The Woman indulged in religion once a week at a church nearby, and took Conradin with her, but to him the church service was an alien rite in the House of Rimmon. Every Thursday, in the dim and musty silence of the tool-shed, he worshipped with mystic and elaborate ceremonial before the wooden hutch where dwelt Sredni Vashtar, the great ferret. Red flowers in their season and scarlet berries in the wintertime were offered at his shrine, for he was a god who laid some special stress on the fierce impatient side of things, as opposed to the Woman's religion, which, as far as Conradin could observe, went to great lengths in the contrary direction. And on great festivals powdered nutmeg was strewn in front of his hutch, an important feature of the offering being that the nutmeg had to be stolen. These festivals were of irregular occurrence, and were chiefly appointed to celebrate some passing event. On one occasion, when Mrs. De Ropp suffered from acute toothache for three days, Conradin kept up the festival during the entire three days, and almost succeeded in persuading himself that Sredni Vashtar was personally responsible for the toothache. If the malady had lasted for another day the supply of nutmeg would have given out.

The Houdan hen was never drawn into the cult of Sredni Vashtar. Conradin had long ago settled that she was an Anabaptist. He did not pretend to have the remotest knowledge as to what an Anabaptist was, but he privately hoped that it was dashing and not very respectable. Mrs. De Ropp was the ground plan on which he based and detested all respectability.

After a while Conradin's absorption in the tool-shed began to attract the notice of his guardian. "It is not good for him to be pottering down there in all weathers," she promptly decided, and at breakfast one morning she announced that the Houdan hen had been sold and taken away overnight. With her short-sighted eyes she peered at Conradin, waiting for an outbreak of rage and sorrow, which she was ready to rebuke with a flow of excellent precepts and reasoning. But Conradin said nothing: there was nothing to be said. Something perhaps in his white set face gave her a momentary qualm, for at tea that afternoon there was toast on the table, a delicacy which she usually banned on the ground that it was bad for him; also because the making of it "gave trouble," a deadly offence in the middle-class feminine eye.

"I thought you liked toast," she exclaimed with an injured air, observing that he did not touch it.

"Sometimes," said Conradin.

In the shed that evening there was an innovation in the worship of the hutch-god. Conradin had been wont to chant his praises; tonight he asked a boon.

"Do one thing for me, Sredni Vashtar."

The thing was not specified. As Sredni Vashtar was a god, he must be supposed to know. And choking back a sob as he looked at that other empty corner, Conradin went back to the world he so hated.

And every night, in the welcome darkness of his bedroom, and every evening in the dusk of the tool-shed, Conradin's bitter litany went up: "Do one thing for me, Sredni Vashtar."

Mrs. De Ropp noticed that the visits to the shed did not cease, and one day she made a further journey of inspection.

"What are you keeping in that locked hutch?" she asked. "I believe it's guinea pigs. I'll have them all cleared away."

Conradin shut his lips tight, but the Woman ransacked his bedroom till she found the carefully hidden key, and forthwith marched down to the shed to complete her discovery. It was a cold afternoon, and Conradin had been bidden to keep to the house. From the farthest window of the dining room the door of the shed could just be seen beyond the corner of the shrubbery, and there Conradin stationed himself. He saw the Woman enter, and then he imagined her opening the door of the sacred hutch and peering down with her short-sighted eyes into the thick straw bed where his god lay hidden. Perhaps she would prod at the straw in her clumsy impatience. And Conradin fervently breathed his prayer for the last time. But he knew as he prayed that he did not believe. He knew that the Woman would come out presently with that pursed smile he loathed so well on her face, and that in an hour or two the gardener would carry away his wonderful god, a god no longer, but a simple brown ferret in a hutch. And he knew that the Woman would triumph always as she triumphed now, and that he would grow ever more sickly under her pestering and domineering and superior wisdom, till one day nothing would matter much more with him, and the doctor would be proved right. And in the sting and misery of his defeat, he began to chant loudly and defiantly the hymn of his threatened idol:

Sredni Vashtar went forth,
His thoughts were red thoughts and his teeth were white.
His enemies called for peace, but he brought them death.
Sredni Vashtar the Beautiful.

And then of a sudden he stopped his chanting and drew closer to the window-pane. The door of the shed still stood ajar as it had been left, and the minutes were slipping by. They were long minutes, but they slipped by nevertheless. He watched the starlings running and flying in little parties across the lawn; he counted them over and over again, with one eye always on that swinging door. A sour-faced maid came in to lay the table for tea, and still Conradin stood and waited and watched. Hope had crept by inches into his heart, and now a look of triumph began to blaze in his eyes that had only known the wistful patience of defeat. Under his breath, with a furtive exultation, he began once again the paean of victory and devastation. And presently his eyes were rewarded: out through that doorway came a long, low, yellow-and-brown beast, with eyes a-blink at the waning daylight, and dark wet stains around the fur of jaws and throat. Conradin dropped on his knees. The great polecat-ferret made its way down to a small brook at the foot of the garden, drank for a moment, then crossed a little plank bridge and was lost to sight in the bushes. Such was the passing of Sredni Vashtar.

"Tea is ready," said the sour-faced maid; "where is the mistress?"

"She went down to the shed some time ago," said Conradin.

And while the maid went to summon her mistress to tea, Conradin fished a toasting-fork out of the sideboard drawer and proceeded to toast himself a piece of bread. And during the toasting of it and the buttering of it with much butter and the slow enjoyment of eating it, Conradin listened to the noises and silences which fell in quick spasms beyond the dining-room door. The loud foolish screaming of the maid, the answering chorus of wondering ejaculations from the kitchen region, the scuttering footsteps and hurried embassies for outside help, and then, after a lull, the scared sobbings and the shuffling tread of those who bore a heavy burden into the house.

"Whoever will break it to the poor child? I couldn't, for the life of me!" exclaimed a shrill voice. And while they debated the matter among themselves, Conradin made himself another piece of toast.

The Chink and the Child
by *Thomas Burke*

It is a tale of love and lovers that they tell in the low-lit Causeway that slinks from West India Dock Road to the dark waste of waters beyond. In Pennyfields, too, you may hear it; and I do not doubt that it is told in far-away Tai-Ping, in Singapore, in Tokio, in Shanghai, and those other gay-lamped haunts of wonder whither the wandering people of Limehouse go and whence they return so casually. It is a tale for tears, and should you hear it in the lilied tongue of the yellow men, it would awaken in you all your pity. In our bald speech it must, unhappily, lose its essential fragrance, that quality that will lift an affair of squalor into the loftier spheres of passion and imagination, beauty and sorrow. It will sound unconvincing, a little . . . you know . . . the kind of thing that is best forgotten. Perhaps . . .

But listen.

It is Battling Burrows, the lightning welter-weight of Shadwell, the box o' tricks, the Tetrarch of the ring, who enters first. Battling Burrows, the pride of Ratcliff, Poplar and Limehouse, and the despair of his manager and backers. For he loved wine, woman and song; and the boxing world held that he couldn't last long on that. There was any amount of money in him for his parasites if only the damned women could be cut out; but again and again would he disappear from his training quarters on the eve of a big fight, to consort with Molly and Dolly, and to drink other things than barley-water and lemon-juice. Wherefore Chuck Lightfoot, his manager, forced him to fight on any and every occasion while he was good and a money-maker, for at any moment the collapse might come, and Chuck would be called upon by his creditors to strip off that "shirt" which at every contest he laid upon his man.

Battling was of a type that is too common in the eastern districts of London; a type that upsets all accepted classifications. He wouldn't be classed. He was a curious mixture of athleticism and degeneracy. He could run like a deer, leap like a greyhound, fight like a machine, and drink like a suction-hose. He was a bully; he had the courage of the high hero. He was an open-air sport; he had the vices of a French decadent.

It was one of his love adventures that properly begins this tale, for the girl had come to Battling one night with a recital of terrible happenings, of an angered parent, of a slammed door. . . . In her arms was a bundle of white rags. Now Battling, like so many sensualists, was also a sentimentalist. He took that bundle of white rags; he paid the girl money to get into the country; and the bundle of white rags had existed in and about his domicile in Pekin Street, Limehouse, for some eleven years. Her position was nondescript; to the casual observer it would seem that she was Battling's relief punch-ball—an unpleasant post for any human creature to occupy, especially if you are a little girl of twelve and the place be the one-room household of the lightning welter-weight. When Battling was cross with his manager . . . well, it is indefensible to strike your manager

8

or to throw chairs at him, if he is a good manager; but to use a dog-whip on a small child is permissible and quite as satisfying; at least, he found it so. On these occasions, then, when very cross with his sparring partners, or over-flushed with victory and juice of the grape, he would flog Lucy. But he was reputed by the boys to be a good fellow. He only whipped the child when he was drunk; and he was only drunk for eight months of the year.

For just over twelve years this bruised little body had crept about Poplar and Limehouse. Always the white face was scarred with red, or black-furrowed with tears; always in her steps and in her look was expectation of dread things. Night after night her sleep was broken by the cheerful Battling's brute voice and violent hands; and terrible were the lessons which life taught her in those few years. Yet, for all the starved face and the transfixed air, there was a lurking beauty about her, a something that called you in the soft curve of her cheek that cried for kisses and was fed with blows, and in the splendid mournfulness that grew in eyes and lips. The brown hair chimed against the pale face, like the rounding of a verse. The blue cotton frock and the broken shoes could not break the loveliness of her slender figure or the shy grace of her movements as she flitted about the squalid alleys of the docks; though in all that region of wasted life and toil and decay, there was not one that noticed her, until . . .

Now there lived in Chinatown, in one lousy room over Mr. Tai Fu's store in Pennyfields, a wandering yellow man named Cheng Huan. Cheng Huan was a poet. He did not realise it. He had never been able to understand why he was unpopular; and he died without knowing. But a poet he was, tinged with the materialism of his race, and in his poor listening heart strange echoes would awake of which he himself was barely conscious. He regarded things differently from other

9

sailors; he felt things more passionately, and things which they felt not at all; so he lived alone instead of at one of the lodging-houses. Every evening he would sit at his window and watch the street. Then, a little later, he would take a jolt of opium at the place at the corner of Formosa Street.

He had come to London by devious ways. He had loafed on the Bund at Shanghai. The fateful intervention of a crimp had landed him on a boat. He got to Cardiff, and sojourned in its Chinatown; thence to Liverpool, to Glasgow; thence, by a ticket from the Asiatics' Aid Society, to Limehouse, where he remained for two reasons—because it cost him nothing to live there, and because he was too lazy to find a boat to take him back to Shanghai.

So he would lounge and smoke cheap cigarettes, and sit at his window, from which point he had many times observed the lyrical Lucy. He noticed her casually. Another day, he observed her, not casually. Later, he looked long at her; later still, he began to watch for her and for that strangely provocative something about the toss of the head and the hang of the little blue skirt as it coyly kissed her knee.

Then that beauty which all Limehouse had missed smote Cheng. Straight to his heart it went, and cried itself into his very blood. Thereafter the spirit of poetry broke her blossoms all about his odorous chamber. Nothing was the same. Pennyfields became a happy-lanterned street, and the monotonous fiddle in the house opposite was the music of his fathers. Bits of old song floated through his mind: little sweet verses of Le Tai-pih, murmuring of plum blossom, rice-field and stream. Day by day he would moon at his window, or shuffle about the streets, lighting to a flame when Lucy would pass and gravely return his quiet regard; and night after night, too, he would dream of a pale, lily-lovely child.

And now the Fates moved swiftly various pieces on their sinister board, and all that followed happened with a speed and precision that showed direction from higher ways.

It was Wednesday night in Limehouse, and for once clear of mist. Out of the coloured darkness of the Causeway stole the muffled wail of reed instruments, and, though every window was closely shuttered, between the joints shot jets of light and stealthy voices, and you could hear the whisper of slippered feet, and the stuttering steps of the satyr and the sadist. It was to the café in the middle of the Causeway, lit by the pallid blue light that is the symbol of China throughout the world, that Cheng Huan came, to take a dish of noodle and some tea. Thence he moved to another house whose stairs ran straight to the street, and above whose doorway a lamp glowed like an evil eye. At this establishment he mostly took his pipe of "chandu" and a brief chat with the keeper of the house, for, although not popular, and very silent, he liked sometimes to be in the presence of his compatriots. Like a figure of a shadowgraph he slid through the door and up the stairs.

The chamber he entered was a bit of the Orient squatting at the portals of the West. It was a well-kept place where one might play a game of fan-tan, or take a shot or so of *li-un*, or purchase other varieties of Oriental delight. It was sunk in a purple dusk, though here and there a lantern stung the gloom. Low couches lay around the walls, and strange men decorated them: Chinese, Japs, Malays, Lascars, with one or two white girls; and sleek, noiseless attendants swam from couch to couch. Away in the far corner sprawled a lank figure in brown shirting, its nerveless fingers curled about the stem of a spent pipe. On one of the lounges a scorbutic nigger sat with a Jewess from Shadwell. Squatting on a table in the centre, beneath one of the lanterns, was a musician with a reed, blinking upon the company like a sly cat and making his melody of six repeated notes.

The atmosphere churned. The dirt of years, tobacco of many growings, opium, betel nut, and moist flesh allied themselves in one grand assault against the nostrils.

As Cheng brooded on his insect-ridden cushion, of a sudden the lantern above the musician was caught by the ribbon of his reed. It danced and flung a hazy radiance on a divan in the shadow. He saw—started—half rose. His heart galloped, and the blood pounded in his quiet veins. Then he dropped again, crouched, and stared.

O lily-flowers and plum blossoms! O silver streams and dim-starred skies! O wine and roses, song and laughter! For there, kneeling on a mass of rugs, mazed and big-eyed, but understanding, was Lucy . . . his Lucy . . . his little maid. Through the dusk she must have felt his intent gaze upon her; for he crouched there, fascinated, staring into the now obscured corner where she knelt.

But the sickness which momentarily gripped him on finding in this place his snowy-breasted pearl passed and gave place to great joy. She was here; he would talk with her. Little English he had, but simple words, those with few gutturals, he had managed to pick up; so he rose, the masterful lover, and, with feline movements, crossed the nightmare chamber to claim his own.

If you wonder how Lucy came to be in this bagnio, the explanation is simple. Battling was in training. He had flogged her that day before starting work; he had then had a few brandies—not many; some eighteen or nineteen—and had locked the door of his room and taken the key. Lucy was, therefore, homeless, and a girl somewhat older than Lucy, so old and so wise, as girls are in that region, saw in her a possible source of revenue. So there they were, and to them appeared Cheng.

From what horrors he saved her that night cannot be told, for her ways were too audaciously childish to hold her long from harm in such a place. What he brought to her was love and death.

For he sat by her. He looked at her—reverently yet

passionately. He touched her—wistfully yet eagerly. He locked a finger in her wondrous hair. She did not start away; she did not tremble. She knew well what she had to be afraid of in that place; but she was not afraid of Cheng. She pierced the mephitic gloom and scanned his face. No, she was not afraid. His yellow hands, his yellow face, his smooth black hair . . . well, he was the first thing that had ever spoken soft words to her; the first thing that had ever laid a hand upon her that was not brutal; the first thing that had deferred in manner towards her as though she, too, had a right to live. She knew his words were sweet, though she did not understand them. Nor can they be set down. Half that he spoke was in village Chinese; the rest in a mangling of English which no distorted spelling could possibly reproduce.

But he drew her back against the cushions and asked her name, and she told him; and he inquired her age, and she told him; and he had then two beautiful words which came easily to his tongue. He repeated them again and again: "Lucia . . . li'l Lucia. . . . Twelve. . . . Twelve." Musical phrases they were, dropping from his lips, and to the child who heard her name pronounced so lovingly, they were the lost heights of melody. She clung to him, and he to her. She held his strong arm in both of hers as they crouched on the divan, and nestled her cheek against his coat.

Well . . . he took her home to his wretched room.

"Li'l Lucia, come-a-home . . . Lucia."

His heart was on fire. As they slipped out of the noisomeness into the night air and crossed the West India Dock Road into Pennyfields, they passed unnoticed. It was late, for one thing, and for another . . . well, nobody cared particularly. His blood rang with soft music and the solemnity of drums, for surely he had found now what for many years he had sought—his world's one flower. Wanderer he was, from Tuan-tsen to Shanghai, Shanghai to Glasgow . . . Cardiff . . .

13

Liverpool . . . London. He had dreamed often of the women of his native land; perchance one of them should be his flower. Women, indeed, there had been. Swatow . . . he had recollections of certain rose-winged hours in coast cities. At many places to which chance had led him a little bird had perched itself upon his heart, but so lightly and for so brief a while as hardly to be felt. But now—now he had found her in this alabaster Cockney child. So that he was glad and had great joy of himself and the blue and silver night, and the harsh flares of the Poplar Hippodrome.

You will observe that he had claimed her, but had not asked himself whether she were of an age for love. The white perfection of the child had captivated every sense. It may be that he forgot that he was in London and not in Tuan-tsen. It may be that he did not care. Of that nothing can be told. All that is known is that his love was a pure and holy thing. Of that we may be sure, for his worst enemies have said it.

Slowly, softly they mounted the stairs to his room, and with almost an obeisance he entered and drew her in. A bank of cloud raced to the east and a full moon thrust a sharp sword of light upon them. Silence lay over all Pennyfields. With a birdlike movement she looked up at him—her face alight, her tiny hands upon his coat—clinging, wondering, trusting. He took her hand and kissed it; repeated the kiss upon her cheek and lip and little bosom, twining his fingers in her hair. Docilely, and echoing the smile of his lemon lips in a way that thrilled him almost to laughter, she returned his kisses impetuously, gladly.

He clasped the nestling to him. Bruised, tearful, with the love of life almost thrashed out of her, she had fluttered to him out of the evil night.

"O li'l Lucia!" And he put soft hands upon her, and smoothed her and crooned over her many gracious things in his flowered speech. So they stood in the moonlight, while she told him the story of her father, of her beatings, and starvings, and unhappiness.

"O li'l Lucia. . . . White Blossom. . . . Twelve. . . . Twelve years old!"

As he spoke, the clock above the Milwall Docks shot twelve crashing notes across the night. When the last echo died, he moved to a cupboard, and from it he drew strange things . . . formless masses of blue and gold, magical things of silk, and a vessel that was surely Aladdin's lamp, and a box of spices. He took these robes and with tender, reverent fingers removed from his White Blossom the besmirched rags that covered her, and robed her again, and led her then to the heap of stuff that was his bed, and bestowed her safely.

For himself, he squatted on the floor before her, holding one grubby little hand. There he crouched all night, under the lyric moon, sleepless, watchful; and sweet content was his. He had fallen into an uncomfortable posture, and his muscles ached intolerably. But she slept, and he dared not move or release her hand lest he awaken her. Weary and trustful, she slept, knowing that the yellow man was kind and that she might sleep with no fear of a steel hand smashing the delicate structure of her dreams.

In the morning, when she awoke, still wearing her blue and yellow silk, she gave a cry of amazement. Cheng had been about. Many times had he glided up and down the two flights of stairs, and now at last his room was prepared for his princess. It was swept and garnished, and was an apartment worthy a maid who is loved by a poet-prince. There was a bead curtain. There were muslins of pink and white. There were four bowls of flowers, clean, clear flowers to gladden the White Blossom and set off her sharp beauty. And there was a bowl of water, and a sweet lotion for the bruise on her cheek.

When she had risen, her prince ministered to her with

rice and egg and tea. Cleansed and robed and calm, she sat before him, perched on the edge of many cushions as on a throne, with all the grace of the child princess in the story. She was a poem. The beauty hidden by neglect and fatigue shone out now more clearly and vividly, and from the head sunning over with curls to the small white feet, now bathed and sandalled, she seemed the living interpretation of a Chinese lyric. And she was his; her sweet self and her prattle, and her bird-like ways were all his own.

Oh, beautifully they loved. For two days he held her. Soft caresses from his yellow hands and long, devout kisses were all their demonstration. Each night he would tend her, as might mother to child; and each night he watched and sometimes slumbered at the foot of her couch.

But now there were those that ran to Battling at his training quarters across the river, with the news that his child had gone with a Chink—a yellow man. And Battling was angry. He discovered parental rights. He discovered indignation. A yellow man after his kid! He'd learn him. Battling did not like men who were not born in the same great country as himself. Particularly he disliked yellow men. His birth and education in Shadwell had taught him that of all creeping things that creep upon the earth the most insidious is the Oriental in the West. And a yellow man and a child. It was . . . as you might say . . . so . . . kind of . . . well, wasn't it? He bellowed that it was "unnacherel." The yeller man would go through it. Yeller! It was his supreme condemnation, his final epithet for all conduct of which he disapproved.

There was no doubt that he was extremely annoyed. He went to the Blue Lantern, in what was once Ratcliff Highway, and thumped the bar, and made all his world agree with him. And when they agreed with him he got angrier still. So that when, a few hours later, he climbed through the ropes at the Netherlands to meet Bud Tuffit for ten rounds, it was Bud's fight all the time, and to that bright boy's astonishment he was the victor on points at the end of the ten. Battling slouched out of the ring, still more determined to let the Chink have it where the chicken had the axe. He left the house with two pals and a black man, and a number of really inspired curses from his manager.

On the evening of the third day, then, Cheng slipped sleepily down the stairs to procure more flowers and more rice. The genial Ho Ling, who keeps the Canton store, held him in talk some little while, and he was gone from his room perhaps half-an-hour. Then he glided back, and climbed with happy feet the forty stairs to his temple of wonder.

With a push of a finger he opened the door, and the blood froze on his cheek; the flowers fell from him. The temple was empty and desolate; White Blossom was gone. The muslin hangings were torn down and trampled underfoot. The flowers had been flung from their bowls about the floor, and the bowls lay in fifty fragments. The joss was smashed. The cupboard had been opened. Rice was scattered here and there. The little straight bed had been jumped upon by brute feet. Everything that could be smashed or violated had been so treated, and—horror of all—the blue and yellow silk robe had been rent in pieces, tied in grotesque knots, and slung derisively about the table legs.

I pray devoutly that you may never suffer what Cheng Huan suffered in that moment. The pangs of death, with no dying; the sickness of the soul which longs to escape and cannot; the imprisoned animal within the breast which struggles madly for a voice and finds none; all the agonies of all the ages—the agonies of every abandoned lover and lost woman, past and to come—all these things were his in that moment.

Then he found voice and gave a great cry, and men from

17

below came up to him; and they told him how the man who boxed had been there with a black man; how he had torn the robes from his child and dragged her down the stairs by her hair; and how he had shouted aloud for Cheng and had vowed to return and deal separately with him.

Now a terrible dignity came to Cheng, and the soul of his great fathers swept over him. He closed the door against them, and fell prostrate over what had been the resting-place of White Blossom. Those without heard strange sounds as of an animal in its last pains; and it was even so. Cheng was dying. The sacrament of his high and holy passion had been profaned; the last sanctuary of the Oriental—his soul dignity—had been assaulted. The love robes had been torn to ribbons, the veil of his temple cut down. Life was no longer possible; and life without his little lady, his White Blossom, was no longer desirable.

Prostrate he lay for the space of some five minutes. Then, in his face all the pride of accepted destiny, he arose. He drew together the little bed. With reverent hands he took the pieces of blue and yellow silk, kissing them and fondling them and placing them about the pillow. Silently he gathered up the flowers and the broken earthenware, and burnt some prayer papers and prepared himself for death.

Now it is the custom among those of the sect of Cheng that the dying shall present love-gifts to their enemies; and when he had set all in order, he gathered his brown canvas coat about him, stole from the house, and set out to find Battling Burrows, bearing under the coat his love-gift to Battling. White Blossom he had no hope of finding. He had heard of Burrows many times; and he judged that, now that she was taken from him, never again would he hold those hands or touch that laughing hair. Nor, if he did, could it change things from what they were. Nothing that was not a dog could live in the face of this sacrilege.

18

As he came before the house in Pekin Street where Battling lived, he murmured gracious prayers. Fortunately, it was a night of thick river mist, and through the enveloping velvet none could observe or challenge him. The main door was open, as are all doors in this district. He writhed across the step, and through to the back room, where again the door yielded to a touch.

Darkness. Darkness and silence, and a sense of frightful things. He peered through it. Then he fumbled under his jacket—found a match—struck it. An inch of candle stood on the mantelshelf. He lit it. He looked round. No sign of Burrows, but . . . Almost before he looked he knew what awaited him. But the sense of finality had kindly stunned him; he could suffer nothing more.

On the table lay a dog-whip. In the corner a belt had been flung. Half across the greasy couch lay White Blossom. A few rags of clothing were about her pale, slim body; her hair hung limp as her limbs; her eyes were closed. As Cheng drew nearer and saw the savage red rails that ran across and across the beloved body, he could not scream—he could not think. He dropped beside the couch. He laid gentle hands upon her, and called soft names. She was warm to the touch. The pulse was still.

Softly, oh, so softly, he bent over the little frame that had enclosed his friend-spirit, and his light kisses fell all about her. Then, with the undirected movements of a sleepwalker, he bestowed the rags decently about her, clasped her in strong arms, and crept silently into the night.

From Pekin Street to Pennyfields it is but a turn or two, and again he passed unobserved as he bore his tired bird back to her nest. He laid her upon the bed, and covered the lily limbs with the blue and yellow silks and strewed upon her a few of the trampled flowers. Then, with more kisses and prayers, he crouched beside her.

19

So, in the ghastly Limehouse morning, they were found—the dead child, and the Chink, kneeling beside her, with a sharp knife gripped in a vicelike hand, its blade far between his ribs.

Meantime, having vented his wrath on his prodigal daughter, Battling, still cross, had returned to the Blue Lantern, and there he stayed with a brandy tumbler in his fist, forgetful of an appointment at Premierland, whereby he should have been in the ring at ten o'clock sharp. For the space of an hour Chuck Lightfoot was going blasphemously to and fro in Poplar, seeking Battling and not finding him, and murmuring, in tearful tones: "Battling—you dammanblasted Battling—where are yeh?"

His opponent was in his corner sure enough, but there was no fight. For Battling lurched from the Blue Lantern to Pekin Street. He lurched into his happy home, and he cursed Lucy, and called for her. And finding no matches, he lurched to where he knew the couch should be, and flopped heavily down.

Now it is a peculiarity of the reptile tribe that its members are impatient of being flopped on without warning. So, when Battling flopped, eighteen inches of writhing gristle upreared itself on the couch, and got home on him as Bud Tuffit had done the night before—one to the ear, one to the throat, and another to the forearm.

Battling went down and out.

And he, too, was found in the morning, with Cheng Huan's love-gift coiled about his neck.

Wash
by William Faulkner

Sutpen stood above the pallet bed on which the mother and child lay. Between the shrunken planking of the wall the early sunlight fell in long pencil strokes, breaking upon his straddled legs and upon the riding whip in his hand, and lay across the still shape of the mother, who lay looking up at him from still, inscrutable, sullen eyes, the child at her side wrapped in a piece of dingy though clean cloth. Behind them an old Negro woman squatted beside the rough hearth where a meager fire smoldered.

"Well, Milly," Sutpen said, "too bad you're not a mare. Then I could give you a decent stall in the stable."

Still the girl on the pallet did not move. She merely continued to look up at him without expression, with a young, sullen, inscrutable face still pale from recent travail. Sutpen moved, bringing into the splintered pencils of sunlight the face of a man of sixty. He said quietly to the squatting Negress, "Griselda foaled this morning."

"Horse or mare?" the Negress said.

"A horse. A damned fine colt. . . . What's this?" He indicated the pallet with the hand which held the whip.

"That un's a mare, I reckon."

"Hah," Sutpen said. "A damned fine colt. Going to be the spit and image of old Rob Roy when I rode him North in '61. Do you remember?"

"Yes, Marster."

"Hah." He glanced back toward the pallet. None could have said if the girl still watched him or not. Again his whip hand indicated the pallet. "Do whatever they need with whatever we've got to do it with." He went out, passing out the crazy doorway and stepping down into the rank weeds (there yet leaned rusting against the corner of the porch the scythe which Wash had borrowed from him three months ago to cut them with) where his horse waited, where Wash stood holding the reins.

When Colonel Sutpen rode away to fight the Yankees, Wash did not go. "I'm looking after the Kernel's place and niggers," he would tell all who asked him and some who had not asked—a gaunt, malaria-ridden man with pale, questioning eyes, who looked about thirty-five, though it was known that he had not only a daughter but an eight-year-old granddaughter as well. This was a lie, as most of them—the few remaining men between eighteen and fifty—to whom he told it, knew, though there were some who believed that he himself really believed it, though even these believed that he had better sense than to put it to the test with Mrs. Sutpen or the Sutpen slaves. Knew better or was just too lazy and shiftless to try it, they said, knowing that his sole connection with the Sutpen plantation lay in the fact that for years now Colonel Sutpen had allowed him to squat in a crazy shack on a slough in the river bottom on the Sutpen place, which Sutpen had built for a fishing lodge in his bachelor days and which had since fallen into dilapidation from disuse, so that now it looked like an aged or sick wild beast crawled terrifically there to drink in the act of dying.

The Sutpen slaves themselves heard of his statement. They laughed. It was not the first time they had laughed at him, calling him white trash behind his back. They began to ask him themselves, in groups, meeting him in the faint road which led up from the slough and the old fish camp, "Why ain't you at de war, white man?"

Pausing, he would look about the ring of black faces and white eyes and teeth behind which derision lurked. "Because I got a daughter and family to keep," he said. "Git out of my road, niggers."

"Niggers?" they repeated; "niggers?" laughing now. "Who him, calling us niggers?"

"Yes," he said. "I ain't got no niggers to look after my folks if I was gone."

"Nor nothing else but dat shack down yon dat Cunnel wouldn't *let* none of us live in."

Now he cursed them; sometimes he rushed at them, snatching up a stick from the ground while they scattered before him, yet seeming to surround him still with that black laughing, derisive, evasive, inescapable, leaving him panting and impotent and raging. Once it happened in the very back yard of the big house itself. This was after bitter news had come down from the Tennessee mountains and from Vicksburg, and Sherman had passed through the plantation, and most of the Negroes had followed him. Almost everything else had gone with the Federal troops, and Mrs. Sutpen had sent word to Wash that he could have the scuppernongs ripening in the arbor in the back yard. This time it was a house servant, one of the few Negroes who remained; this time the Negress had to retreat up the kitchen steps, where she turned. "Stop right dar, white man. Stop right whar you is. You ain't never crossed dese steps whilst Cunnel here, and you ain't ghy' do hit now."

This was true. But there was this of a kind of pride: he had never tried to enter the big house, even though he believed that if he had, Sutpen would have received him, permitted him. "But I ain't going to give no black nigger the chance to tell me I can't go nowhere," he said to himself. "I ain't even going to give Kernel the chance to have to cuss a nigger on my account." This, though he and Sutpen had spent more than one afternoon together on those rare Sundays when there would be no company in the house. Perhaps his mind knew that it was because Sutpen had nothing else to do, being a man who could not bear his own company. Yet the fact remained that the two of them would spend whole afternoons in the scuppernong arbor, Sutpen in the hammock and Wash squatting against a post, a pail of cistern water between them, taking drink for drink from the same demijohn. Meanwhile on weekdays he would see the fine figure of the man—they were the same age almost to a day, though neither of them (perhaps because Wash had a grandchild while Sutpen's son was a youth in school) ever thought of himself as being so—on the fine figure of the black stallion, galloping about the plantation. For that moment his heart would be quiet and proud. It would seem to him that that world in which Negroes, whom the Bible told him had been created and cursed by God to be brute and vassal to all men of white skin, were better found and housed and even clothed than he and his; that world in which he sensed always about him mocking echoes of black laughter was but a dream and an illusion, and that the actual world was this one across which his own lonely apotheosis seemed to gallop on the black thoroughbred, thinking how the Book said also that all men were created in the image of God and hence all men made the same image in God's eyes, at least; so that he could say, as though speaking of himself, "A fine proud man. If God Himself was to come down and ride the natural earth, that's what He would aim to look like."

Sutpen returned in 1865, on the black stallion. He

seemed to have aged ten years. His son had been killed in action the same winter in which his wife had died. He returned with his citation for gallantry from the hand of General Lee to a ruined plantation, where for a year now his daughter had subsisted partially on the meager bounty of the man to whom fifteen years ago he had granted permission to live in that tumbledown fishing camp whose very existence he had at the time forgotten. Wash was there to meet him, unchanged: still gaunt, still ageless, with his pale, questioning gaze, his air diffident, a little servile, a little familiar. "Well, Kernel," Wash said, "they kilt us, but they ain't whupped us yit, air they?"

That was the tenor of their conversation for the next five years. It was inferior whisky which they drank now together from a stoneware jug, and it was not in the scuppernong arbor. It was in the rear of the little store which Sutpen managed to set up on the highroad: a frame shelved room where, with Wash for clerk and porter, he dispensed kerosene and staple foodstuffs and stale gaudy candy and cheap beads and ribbons to Negroes or poor whites of Wash's own kind, who came afoot or on gaunt mules to haggle tediously for dimes and quarters with a man who at one time could gallop (the black stallion was still alive; the stable in which his jealous get lived was in better repair than the house where the master himself lived) for ten miles across his own fertile land and who had led troops gallantly in battle; until Sutpen in fury would empty the store, close and lock the doors from the inside. Then he and Wash would repair to the rear and the jug. But the talk would not be quiet now, as when Sutpen lay in the hammock, delivering an arrogant monologue while Wash squatted guffawing against his post. They both sat now, though Sutpen had the single chair while Wash used whatever box or keg was handy, and even this for just a little while, because soon Sutpen would reach that stage of impotent and furious undefeat in which he would rise, swaying and plunging, and declare again that he would take his pistol and the black stallion and ride single-handed into Washington and kill Lincoln, dead now, and Sherman, now a private citizen. "Kill them!" he would shout. "Shoot them down like the dogs they are——"

"Sho, Kernel; sho, Kernel," Wash would say, catching Sutpen as he fell. Then he would commandeer the first passing wagon or, lacking that, he would walk the mile to the nearest neighbor and borrow one and return and carry Sutpen home. He entered the house now. He had been doing so for a long time, taking Sutpen home in whatever borrowed wagon might be, talking him into locomotion with cajoling murmurs as though he were a horse, a stallion himself. The daughter would meet them and hold open the door without a word. He would carry his burden through the once white formal entrance, surmounted by a fanlight imported piece by piece from Europe and with a board now nailed over a missing pane, across a velvet carpet from which all nap was now gone, and up a formal stairs, now but a fading ghost of bare boards between two strips of fading paint, and into the bedroom. It would be dusk by now, and he would let his burden sprawl onto the bed and undress it and then he would sit quietly in a chair beside. After a time the daughter would come to the door. "We're all right now," he would tell her. "Don't you worry none, Miss Judith."

Then it would become dark, and after a while he would lie down on the floor beside the bed, though not to sleep, because after a time—sometimes before midnight—the man on the bed would stir and groan and then speak. "Wash?"

"Hyer I am, Kernel. You go back to sleep. We ain't whupped yit, air we? Me and you kin do hit."

Even then he had already seen the ribbon about his granddaughter's waist. She was now fifteen, already mature, after the early way of her kind. He knew where the ribbon came from; he had been seeing it and its kind daily for three years, even if she had lied about where she got it, which she did not, at once bold, sullen, and fearful. "Sho now," he said. "Ef Kernel wants to give hit to you, I hope you minded to thank him."

His heart was quiet, even when he saw the dress, watching her secret, defiant, frightened face when she told him that Miss Judith, the daughter, had helped her to make it. But he was quite grave when he approached Sutpen after they closed the store that afternoon, following the other to the rear.

"Get the jug," Sutpen directed.

"Wait," Wash said. "Not yit for a minute."

Neither did Sutpen deny the dress. "What about it?" he said.

But Wash met his arrogant stare; he spoke quietly. "I've knowed you for going on twenty years. I ain't never yit denied to do what you told me to do. And I'm a man nigh sixty. And she ain't nothing but a fifteen-year-old gal."

"Meaning that I'd harm a girl? I, a man as old as you are?"

"If you was ara other man, I'd say you was as old as me. And old or no old, I wouldn't let her keep that dress nor nothing else that come from your hand. But you are different."

"How different?" But Wash merely looked at him with his pale, questioning, sober eyes. "So that's why you are afraid of me?"

Now Wash's gaze no longer questioned. It was tranquil, serene. "I ain't afraid. Because you air brave. It ain't that you were a brave man at one minute or day of your life and got a paper to show hit from General Lee. But you air brave, the same as you air alive and breathing. That's where hit's different. Hit don't need no ticket from nobody to tell me that. And I know that whatever you handle or tech, whether hit's a regiment of men or a ignorant gal or just a hound dog, that you will make hit right."

Now it was Sutpen who looked away, turning suddenly, brusquely. "Get the jug," he said sharply.

"Sho, Kernel," Wash said.

So on that Sunday dawn two years later, having watched the Negro midwife, which he had walked three miles to fetch, enter the crazy door beyond which his granddaughter lay wailing, his heart was still quiet though concerned. He knew what they had been saying—the Negroes in cabins about the land, the white men who loafed all day long about the store, watching quietly the three of them: Sutpen, himself, his granddaughter with her air of brazen and shrinking defiance as her condition became daily more and more obvious, like three actors that came and went upon a stage. "I know what they say to one another," he thought. "I can almost hyear them: *Wash Jones has fixed old Sutpen at last. Hit taken him twenty years, but he has done hit at last.*"

It would be dawn after a while, though not yet. From the house, where the lamp shone dim beyond the warped doorframe, his granddaughter's voice came steadily as though run by a clock, while thinking went slowly and terrifically, fumbling, involved somehow with a sound of galloping hooves, until there broke suddenly free in mid-gallop the fine proud figure of the man on the fine proud stallion, galloping; and then that at which thinking fumbled, broke free too and quite clear, not in justification or even explanation, but as the apotheosis, lonely, explicable, beyond all fouling by human touch: "He is bigger than all them Yankees that kilt his son and his wife and taken his niggers and ruined his land, bigger than this hyer durn country that he fit for and that has denied him into keeping a little country store; bigger than the denial which hit helt to his lips like the bitter cup in the Book. And how could I have lived this nigh to him for twenty years without being teched and changed by him? Maybe I ain't as big as him and maybe I ain't done none of the galloping. But at least I done been drug along. Me and him kin do hit, if so be he will show me what he aims for me to do."

Then it was dawn. Suddenly he could see the house, and the old Negress in the door looking at him. Then he realized that his granddaughter's voice had ceased. "It's a girl," the Negress said. "You can go tell him if you want to." She reëntered the house.

"A girl," he repeated; "a girl"; in astonishment, hearing the galloping hooves, seeing the proud galloping figure emerge again. He seemed to watch it pass, galloping through avatars which marked the accumulation of years, time, to the climax where it galloped beneath a brandished saber and a shot-torn flag rushing down a sky in color like thunderous sulphur, thinking for the first time in his life that perhaps Sutpen was an old man like himself. "Gittin a gal," he thought in that astonishment; then he thought with the pleased surprise of a child: "Yes, sir. Be dawg if I ain't lived to be a great-grandpaw after all."

He entered the house. He moved clumsily, on tiptoe, as if he no longer lived there, as if the infant which had just drawn breath and cried in light had dispossessed him, be it of his own blood too though it might. But even above the pallet he could see little save the blur of his granddaughter's exhausted face. Then the Negress squatting at the hearth spoke, "You better gawn tell him if you going to. Hit's daylight now."

But this was not necessary. He had no more than turned the corner of the porch where the scythe leaned which he had borrowed three months ago to clear away the weeds through which he walked, when Sutpen himself rode up on the old stallion. He did not wonder how Sutpen had got the word. He took it for granted that this was what had brought the other out at this hour on Sunday morning, and he stood while the other dismounted, and he took the reins from Sutpen's hand, an expression on his gaunt face almost imbecile with a kind of weary triumph, saying, "Hit's a gal, Kernel. I be dawg if you ain't as old as I am——" until Sutpen passed him and entered the house. He stood there with the reins in his hand and heard Sutpen cross the floor to the pallet. He heard what Sutpen said, and something seemed to stop dead in him before going on.

The sun was now up, the swift sun of Mississippi latitudes, and it seemed to him that he stood beneath a strange sky, in a strange scene, familiar only as things are familiar in dreams, like the dreams of falling to one who has never climbed. "I kain't have heard what I thought I heard," he thought quietly. "I know I kain't." Yet the voice, the familiar voice which had said the words was still speaking, talking now to the old Negress about a colt foaled that morning. "That's why he was up so early," he thought. "That was hit. Hit ain't me and mine. Hit ain't even hisn that got him outen bed."

Sutpen emerged. He descended into the weeds, moving with that heavy deliberation which would have been haste when he was younger. He had not yet looked full at Wash. He said, "Dicey will stay and tend to her. You better——" Then he seemed to see Wash facing him and paused. "What?" he said.

"You said——" To his own ears Wash's voice sounded flat and ducklike, like a deaf man's. "You said if she was a mare, you could give her a good stall in the stable."

"Well?" Sutpen said. His eyes widened and narrowed, almost like a man's fists flexing and shutting, as Wash began to advance toward him, stooping a little. Very astonishment kept Sutpen still for the moment, watching that man whom in twenty years he had no more known to make any motion save at command than he had the horse which he rode. Again his eyes narrowed and widened; without moving he seemed to rear suddenly upright. "Stand back," he said suddenly and sharply. "Don't you touch me."

"I'm going to tech you, Kernel," Wash said in that flat, quiet, almost soft voice, advancing.

Sutpen raised the hand which held the riding whip; the old Negress peered around the crazy door with her black gargoyle face of a worn gnome. "Stand back, Wash," Sutpen said. Then he struck. The old Negress leaped down into the weeds with the agility of a goat and fled. Sutpen slashed Wash again across the face with the whip, striking him to his knees. When Wash rose and advanced once more he held in his hands the scythe which he had borrowed from Sutpen three months ago and which Sutpen would never need again.

When he reëntered the house his granddaughter stirred on the pallet bed and called his name fretfully. "What was that?" she said.

"What was what, honey?"

"That ere racket out there."

" 'Twarn't nothing," he said gently. He knelt and touched her hot forehead clumsily. "Do you want ara thing?"

"I want a sup of water," she said querulously. "I been laying here wanting a sup of water a long time, but don't nobody care enough to pay me no mind."

"Sho now," he said soothingly. He rose stiffly and fetched the dipper of water and raised her head to drink and laid her back and watched her turn to the child with an absolutely stonelike face. But a moment later he saw that she was crying quietly. "Now, now," he said, "I wouldn't do that. Old Dicey says hit's a right fine gal. Hit's all right now. Hit's all over now. Hit ain't no need to cry now."

But she continued to cry quietly, almost sullenly, and he

rose again and stood uncomfortably above the pallet for a time, thinking as he had thought when his own wife lay so and then his daughter in turn: "Women. Hit's a mystry to me. They seem to want em, and yit when they git em they cry about hit. Hit's a mystry to me. To ara man." Then he moved away and drew a chair up to the window and sat down.

Through all that long, bright, sunny forenoon he sat at the window, waiting. Now and then he rose and tiptoed to the pallet. But his granddaughter slept now, her face sullen and calm and weary, the child in the crook of her arm. Then he returned to the chair and sat again, waiting, wondering why it took them so long, until he remembered that it was Sunday. He was sitting there at mid-afternoon when a half-grown white boy came around the corner of the house upon the body and gave a choked cry and looked up and glared for a mesmerized instant at Wash in the window before he turned and fled. Then Wash rose and tiptoed again to the pallet.

The granddaughter was awake now, wakened perhaps by the boy's cry without hearing it. "Milly," he said, "air you hungry?" She didn't answer, turning her face away. He built up the fire on the hearth and cooked the food which he had brought home the day before: fatback it was, and cold corn pone; he poured water into the stale coffee pot and heated it. But she would not eat when he carried the plate to her, so he ate himself, quietly, alone, and left the dishes as they were and returned to the window.

Now he seemed to sense, feel, the men who would be gathering with horses and guns and dogs—the curious, and the vengeful: men of Sutpen's own kind, who had made the company about Sutpen's table in the time when Wash himself had yet to approach nearer to the house than the scuppernong arbor—men who had also shown the lesser ones how to fight in battle, who maybe also had signed papers from the generals saying that they were among the first of the brave; who had also galloped in the old days arrogant and proud on the fine horses across the fine plantations—symbols also of admiration and hope; instruments too of despair and grief.

That was whom they would expect him to run from. It seemed to him that he had no more to run from than he had to run to. If he ran, he would merely be fleeing one set of bragging and evil shadows for another just like them, since they were all of a kind throughout all the earth which he knew, and he was old, too old to flee far even if he were to flee. He could never escape them, no matter how much or how far he ran: a man going on sixty could not run that far. Not far enough to escape beyond the boundaries of earth where such men lived, set the order and the rule of living. It seemed to him that he now saw for the first time, after five years, how it was that Yankees or any other living armies had managed to whip them: the gallant, the proud, the brave; the acknowledged and chosen best among them all to carry courage and honor and pride. Maybe if he had gone to the war with them he would have discovered them sooner. But if he had discovered them sooner, what would he have done with his life since? How could he have borne to remember for five years what his life had been before?

Now it was getting toward sunset. The child had been crying; when he went to the pallet he saw his granddaughter nursing it, her face still bemused, sullen, inscrutable. "Air you hungry yit?" he said.

"I don't want nothing."

"You ought to eat."

This time she did not answer at all, looking down at the child. He returned to his chair and found that the sun had set. "Hit kain't be much longer," he thought. He could feel them quite near now, the curious and the vengeful. He could even seem to hear what they were saying about him, the undercurrent of believing beyond the immediate fury: *Old Wash Jones he come a tumble at last. He thought he had Sutpen, but Sutpen fooled him. He thought he had Kernel where he would have to marry the gal or pay up. And Kernel refused.* "But I never expected that, Kernel!" he cried aloud, catching himself at the sound of his own voice, glancing quickly back to find his granddaughter watching him.

"Who you talking to now?" she said.

"Hit ain't nothing. I was just thinking and talked out before I knowed hit."

Her face was becoming indistinct again, again a sullen blur in the twilight. "I reckon so. I reckon you'll have to holler louder than that before he'll hear you, up yonder at that house. And I reckon you'll need to do more than holler before you get him down here too."

"Sho now," he said. "Don't you worry none." But already thinking was going smoothly on: "You know I never. You know how I ain't never expected or asked nothing from ara living man but what I expected from you. And I never asked that, I didn't think hit would need. I said, *I don't need to. What need has a fellow like Wash Jones to question or doubt the man that General Lee himself says in a handwrote ticket that he was brave?* Brave," he thought. "Better if nara one of them had never rid back home in '65"; thinking *Better if his kind and mine too had never drawn the breath of life on this earth. Better that all who remain of us be blasted from the face of earth than that another Wash Jones should see his whole life shredded from him and shrivel away like a dried shuck thrown onto the fire.*

He ceased, became still. He heard the horses, suddenly and plainly; presently he saw the lantern and the movement of men, the glint of gun barrels, in its moving light. Yet he did not stir. It was quite dark now, and he listened to the voices and the sounds of underbrush as they surrounded the house. The lantern itself came on; its light fell upon the quiet body in the weeds and stopped, the horses tall and shadowy. A man descended and stooped in the lantern light, above the body. He held a pistol; he rose and faced the house. "Jones," he said.

"I'm here," Wash said quietly from the window. "That you, Major?"

"Come out."

"Sho," he said quietly. "I just want to see to my granddaughter."

"We'll see to her. Come on out."

"Sho, Major. Just a minute."

"Show a light. Light your lamp."

"Sho. In just a minute." They could hear his voice retreat into the house, though they could not see him as he went swiftly to the crack in the chimney where he kept the butcher knife: the one thing in his slovenly life and house in which he took pride, since it was razor sharp. He approached the pallet, his granddaughter's voice:

"Who is it? Light the lamp, grandpaw."

"Hit won't need no light, honey. Hit won't take but a minute," he said, kneeling, fumbling toward her voice, whispering now. "Where air you?"

"Right here," she said fretfully. "Where would I be? What is . . ." His hand touched her face. "What is . . . Grandpaw! Grand . . ."

"Jones!" the sheriff said. "Come out of there!"

"In just a minute, Major," he said. Now he rose and moved swiftly. He knew where in the dark the can of kerosene was, just as he knew that it was full, since it was not two days ago that he had filled it at the store and held it there until he got a ride home with it, since the five gallons were heavy. There were still coals on the hearth; besides, the crazy building itself was like tinder: the coals, the hearth,

35

the walls exploding in a single blue glare. Against it the waiting men saw him in a wild instant springing toward them with the lifted scythe before the horses reared and whirled. They checked the horses and turned them back toward the glare, yet still in wild relief against it the gaunt figure ran toward them with the lifted scythe.

"Jones!" the sheriff shouted. "Stop! Stop, or I'll shoot. Jones! *Jones!*" Yet still the gaunt, furious figure came on against the glare and roar of the flames. With the scythe lifted, it bore down upon them, upon the wild glaring eyes of the horses and the swinging glints of gun barrels, without any cry, any sound.

Mary Postgate
by Rudyard Kipling

Of Miss Mary Postgate, Lady McCausland wrote that she was 'thoroughly conscientious, tidy, companionable, and ladylike. I am very sorry to part with her, and shall always be interested in her welfare.'

Miss Fowler engaged her on this recommendation, and, to her surprise, for she had had experience of companions, found that it was true. Miss Fowler was nearer sixty than fifty at the time, but though she needed care, she did not exhaust her attendant's vitality. On the contrary, she gave out, stimulatingly and with reminiscences. Her father had been a minor Court official in the days when the Great Exhibition of 1851 had just set its seal on Civilisation made perfect. Some of Miss Fowler's tales, none the less, were not always for the young. Mary was not young, and though her speech was as colourless as her eyes or her hair, she was never shocked. She listened unflinchingly to everyone; said at the end, 'How interesting!' or 'How shocking!' as the case might be, and never again referred to it, for she prided herself on a trained mind, which 'did not dwell on these things.' She was, too, a

treasure at domestic accounts, for which the village trades-
men, with their weekly books, loved her not. Otherwise she
had no enemies; provoked no jealousy even among the
plainest; neither gossip nor slander had ever been traced to
her; she supplied the odd place at the Rector's or the
Doctor's table at half an hour's notice; she was a sort of
public aunt to very many small children of the village street,
whose parents, while accepting everything, would have
been swift to resent what they called 'patronage'; she served
on the Village Nursing Committee as Miss Fowler's nominee
when Miss Fowler was crippled by rheumatoid arthritis, and
came out of six months' fortnightly meetings equally re-
spected by all the cliques.

And when Fate threw Miss Fowler's nephew, an unlovely
orphan of eleven, on Miss Fowler's hands, Mary Postgate
stood to her share of the business of education as practised
in private and public schools. She checked printed clothes-
lists and unitemised bills of extras; wrote to Head and House
masters, matrons, nurses and doctors; and grieved or re-
joiced over half-term reports. Young Wyndham Fowler re-
paid her in his holidays by calling her 'Gatepost,' 'Postey,' or
'Packthread,' by thumping her between her narrow shoulders, or by chasing her, bleating, round the garden, her large
mouth open, her large nose high in air, at a stiff-necked
shamble very like a camel's. Later on he filled the house with
clamour, argument, and harangues as to his personal needs,
likes and dislikes, and the limitations of 'you women,'
reducing Mary to tears of physical fatigue, or, when he chose
to be humourous, of helpless laughter. At crises, which
multiplied as he grew older, she was his ambassadress and
his interpretress to Miss Fowler, who had no large sympathy
with the young; a vote in his interest at the councils on his
future; his sewing-woman, strictly accountable for mislaid
boots and garments; always his butt and his slave.

And when he decided to become a solicitor, and had entered an office in London; when his greeting had changed from 'Hullo, Postey, you old beast,' to 'Mornin', Packthread,' there came a war which, unlike all wars that Mary could remember, did not stay decently outside England and in the newspapers, but intruded on the lives of people whom she knew. As she said to Miss Fowler, it was 'most vexatious.' It took the Rector's son who was going into business with his elder brother; it took the Colonel's nephew on the eve of fruit-farming in Canada; it took Mrs. Grant's son who, his mother said, was devoted to the ministry; and, very early indeed, it took Wynn Fowler, who announced on a postcard that he had joined the Flying Corps and wanted a cardigan waistcoat.

'He must go, and he must have the waistcoat,' said Miss Fowler. So Mary got the proper-sized needles and wool, while Miss Fowler told the men of her establishment—two gardeners and an odd man, aged sixty—that those who could join the Army had better do so. The gardeners left. Cheape, the odd man, stayed on, and was promoted to the gardener's cottage. The cook, scorning to be limited in luxuries, also left, after a spirited scene with Miss Fowler, and took the housemaid with her. Miss Fowler gazetted Nellie, Cheape's seventeen-year-old daughter, to the vacant post; Mrs. Cheape to the rank of cook, with occasional cleaning bouts; and the reduced establishment moved forward smoothly.

Wynn demanded an increase in his allowance. Miss Fowler, who always looked facts in the face, said, 'He must have it. The chances are he won't live long to draw it, and if three hundred makes him happy——'

Wynn was grateful, and came over, in his tight-buttoned uniform, to say so. His training centre was not thirty miles away, and his talk was so technical that it had to be ex-

plained by charts of the various types of machines. He gave
Mary such a chart.

'And you'd better study it, Postey,' he said. 'You'll be
seeing a lot of 'em soon.' So Mary studied the chart, but
when Wynn next arrived to swell and exalt himself before his
womenfolk, she failed badly in cross-examination, and he
rated her as in the old days.

'You *look* more or less like a human being,' he said in his
new Service voice. 'You *must* have had a brain at some time
in your past. What have you done with it? Where d'you keep
it? A sheep would know more than you do, Postey. You're
lamentable. You are less use than an empty tin can, you
dowey old cassowary.'

'I suppose that's how your superior officer talks to *you?*'
said Miss Fowler from her chair.

'But Postey doesn't mind,' Wynn replied. 'Do you,
Packthread?'

'Why? Was Wynn saying anything? I shall get this right
next time you come,' she muttered, and knitted her pale
brows again over the diagrams of Taubes, Farmans, and
Zeppelins.

In a few weeks the mere land and sea battles which she
read to Miss Fowler after breakfast passed her like idle
breath. Her heart and her interest were high in the air with
Wynn, who had finished 'rolling' (whatever that might be)
and had gone on from a 'taxi' to a machine more or less his
own. One morning it circled over their very chimneys,
alighted on Vegg's Heath, almost outside the garden gate,
and Wynn came in, blue with cold, shouting for food. He and
she drew Miss Fowler's bath-chair, as they had often done,
along the Heath foot-path to look at the biplane. Mary
observed that 'it smelt very badly.'

'Postey, I believe you think with your nose,' said Wynn. 'I
know you don't with your mind. Now, what type's that?'

'I'll go and get the chart,' said Mary.

'You're hopeless! You haven't the mental capacity of a white mouse,' he cried, and explained the dials and the sockets for bomb-dropping till it was time to mount and ride the wet clouds once more.

'Ah!' said Mary, as the stinking thing flared upward. 'Wait till our Flying Corps gets to work! Wynn says it's much safer than in the trenches.'

'I wonder,' said Miss Fowler. 'Tell Cheape to come and tow me home again.'

'It's all downhill. I can do it,' said Mary, 'if you put the brake on.' She laid her lean self against the pushing-bar, and home they trundled.

'Now, be careful you aren't heated and catch a chill,' said overdressed Miss Fowler.

'Nothing makes me perspire,' said Mary. As she bumped the chair under the porch she straightened her long back. The exertion had given her a colour, and the wind had loosened a wisp of hair across her forehead. Miss Fowler glanced at her.

'What do you ever think of, Mary?' she demanded suddenly.

'Oh, Wynn says he wants another three pairs of stockings—as thick as we can make them.'

'Yes. But I mean the things that women think about. Here you are, more than forty——'

'Forty-four,' said truthful Mary.

'Well?'

'Well?' Mary offered Miss Fowler her shoulder as usual.

'And you've been with me ten years now.'

'Let's see,' said Mary. 'Wynn was eleven when he came. He's twenty now, and I came two years before that. It must be eleven.'

'Eleven! And you've never told me anything that matters

41

in all that while. Looking back, it seems to me that *I've* done all the talking.'

'I'm afraid I'm not much of a conversationalist. As Wynn says, I haven't the mind. Let me take your hat.'

Miss Fowler, moving stiffly from the hip, stamped her rubber-tipped stick on the tiled hall floor. 'Mary, aren't you *anything* except a companion? Would you *ever* have been anything except a companion?'

Mary hung up the garden hat on its proper peg. 'No,' she said after consideration. 'I don't imagine I ever should. But I've no imagination, I'm afraid.'

She fetched Miss Fowler her eleven-o'clock glass of Contrexeville.

That was the wet December when it rained six inches to the month, and the women went abroad as little as might be. Wynn's flying chariot visited them several times, and for two mornings (he had warned her by postcard) Mary heard the thresh of his propellers at dawn. The second time she ran to the window and stared at the whitening sky. A little blur passed overhead. She lifted her lean arms towards it.

That evening at six o'clock there came an announcement in an official envelope that Second Lieutenant W. Fowler had been killed during a trial flight. Death was instantaneous. She read it and carried it to Miss Fowler.

'I never expected anything else,' said Miss Fowler; 'but I'm sorry it happened before he had done anything.'

The room was whirling round Mary Postgate, but she found herself quite steady in the midst of it.

'Yes,' she said. 'It's a great pity he didn't die in action after he had killed somebody.'

'He was killed instantly. That's one comfort,' Miss Fowler went on.

'But Wynn says the shock of a fall kills a man at once—whatever happens to the tanks,' quoted Mary.

The room was coming to rest now. She heard Miss Fowler

say impatiently, 'But why can't we cry, Mary?' and herself replying, 'There's nothing to cry for. He has done his duty as much as Mrs. Grant's son did.'

'And when he died, *she* came and cried all the morning,' said Miss Fowler. 'This only makes me feel tired—terribly tired. Will you help me to bed, please, Mary?—And I think I'd like the hot-water bottle.'

So Mary helped her and sat beside, talking of Wynn in his riotous youth.

'I believe,' said Miss Fowler suddenly, 'that old people and young people slip from under a stroke like this. The middle-aged feel it most.'

'I expect that's true,' said Mary, rising. 'I'm going to put away the things in his room now. Shall we wear mourning?'

'Certainly not,' said Miss Fowler. 'Except, of course, at the funeral. I can't go. You will. I want you to arrange about his being buried here. What a blessing it didn't happen at Salisbury!'

Everyone, from the Authorities of the Flying Corps to the Rector, was most kind and sympathetic. Mary found herself for the moment in a world where bodies were in the habit of being despatched by all sorts of conveyances to all sorts of places. And at the funeral two young men in buttoned-up uniforms stood beside the grave and spoke to her afterwards.

'You're Miss Postgate, aren't you?' said one. 'Fowler told me about you. He was a good chap—a first-class fellow—a great loss.'

'Great loss!' growled his companion. 'We're all awfully sorry.'

'How high did he fall from?' Mary whispered.

'Pretty nearly four thousand feet, I should think, didn't he? You were up that day, Monkey?'

'All of that,' the other child replied. 'My bar made three thousand, and I wasn't as high as him by a lot.'

'Then *that's* all right,' said Mary. 'Thank you very much.'

They moved away as Mrs. Grant flung herself weeping on Mary's flat chest, under the lych-gate, and cried, '*I* know how it feels! *I* know how it feels!'

'But both his parents are dead,' Mary returned, as she fended her off. 'Perhaps they've all met by now,' she added vaguely as she escaped towards the coach.

'I've thought of that too,' wailed Mrs. Grant; 'but then he'll be practically a stranger to them. Quite embarrassing!'

Mary faithfully reported every detail of the ceremony to Miss Fowler, who, when she described Mrs. Grant's outburst, laughed aloud.

'Oh, how Wynn would have enjoyed it! He was always utterly unreliable at funerals. D'you remember——' And they talked of him again, each piecing out the other's gaps. 'And now,' said Miss Fowler, 'we'll pull up the blinds and we'll have a general tidy. That always does us good. Have you seen to Wynn's things?'

'Everything—since he first came,' said Mary. 'He was never destructive—even with his toys.'

They faced that neat room.

'It can't be natural not to cry,' Mary said at last. 'I'm *so* afraid you'll have a reaction.'

'As I told you, we old people slip from under the stroke. It's you I'm afraid for. Have you cried yet?'

'I can't. It only makes me angry with the Germans.'

'That's sheer waste of vitality,' said Miss Fowler. 'We must live till the war's finished.' She opened a full wardrobe. 'Now, I've been thinking things over. This is my plan. All his civilian clothes can be given away—Belgian refugees, and so on.'

Mary nodded. 'Boots, collars, and gloves?'

'Yes. We don't need to keep anything except his cap and belt.'

'They came back yesterday with his Flying Corps clothes'—Mary pointed to a roll on the little iron bed.

44

'Ah, but keep his Service things. Someone may be glad of them later. Do you remember his sizes?'

'Five feet eight and a half; thirty-six inches round the chest. But he told me he's just put on an inch and a half. I'll mark it on a label and tie it on his sleeping-bag.'

'So that disposes of *that*,' said Miss Fowler, tapping the palm of one hand with the ringed third finger of the other. 'What waste it all is! We'll get his old school trunk tomorrow and pack his civilian clothes.'

'And the rest?' said Mary. 'His books and pictures and the games and the toys—and—and the rest?'

'My plan is to burn every single thing,' said Miss Fowler. 'Then we shall know where they are and no one can handle them afterwards. What do you think?'

'I think that would be much the best,' said Mary. 'But there's such a lot of them.'

'We'll burn them in the destructor,' said Miss Fowler.

This was an open-air furnace for the consumption of refuse; a little circular four-foot tower of pierced brick over an iron grating. Miss Fowler had noticed the design in a gardening journal years ago, and had had it built at the bottom of the garden. It suited her tidy soul, for it saved unsightly rubbish-heaps, and the ashes lightened the stiff clay soil.

Mary considered for a moment, saw her way clear, and nodded again. They spent the evening putting away well-remembered civilian suits, underclothes that Mary had marked, and the regiments of very gaudy socks and ties. A second trunk was needed, and, after that, a little packing-case, and it was late next day when Cheape and the local carrier lifted them to the cart. The Rector luckily knew of a friend's son, about five feet eight and a half inches high, to whom a complete Flying Corps outfit would be most accept-able, and sent his gardener's son down with a barrow to take delivery of it. The cap was hung up in Miss Fowler's bedroom, the belt in Miss Postgate's; for, as Miss Fowler said, they had no desire to make tea-party talk of them.

'That disposes of *that*,' said Miss Fowler. 'I'll leave the rest to you, Mary. I can't run up and down the garden. You'd better take the big clothes-basket and get Nellie to help you.'

'I shall take the wheelbarrow and do it myself,' said Mary, and for once in her life closed her mouth.

Miss Fowler, in moments of irritation, had called Mary deadly methodical. She put on her oldest waterproof and gardening-hat and her ever-slipping goloshes, for the weather was on the edge of more rain. She gathered fire-lighters from the kitchen, a half-scuttle of coals, and a faggot of brushwood. These she wheeled in the barrow down the mossed paths to the dank little laurel shrubbery where the destructor stood under the drip of three oaks. She climbed the wire fence into the Rector's glebe just behind, and from his tenant's rick pulled two large armfuls of good hay, which she spread neatly on the fire-bars. Next, journey by journey, passing Miss Fowler's white face at the morning-room window each time, she brought down in the towel-covered clothes-basket, on the wheelbarrow, thumbed and used Hentys, Marryats, Levers, Stevensons, Baroness Orczys, Garvices, schoolbooks, and atlases, unrelated piles of the *Motor Cyclist*, the *Light Car*, and catalogues of Olympia Exhibitions; the remnants of a fleet of sailing-ships from ninepenny cutters to a three-guinea yacht; a prep.-school dressing-gown; bats from three-and-sixpence to twenty-four shillings; cricket and tennis balls; disintegrated steam and clockwork locomotives with their twisted rails; a grey and red tin model of a submarine; a dumb gramophone and cracked records; golf-clubs that had to be broken across the knee, like his walking-sticks, and an assegai; photographs of private and public school cricket and football elevens, and his O.T.C. on the line of march; kodaks, and film-rolls; some pewters, and one real silver cup, for boxing competitions and Junior Hurdles; sheaves of school photographs; Miss Fowler's photograph; her own which he had borne off in fun and (good care she took not to ask!) had never returned; a playbox with a secret drawer; a load of flannels, belts, and jerseys, and a pair of spiked shoes unearthed in the attic; a packet of all the letters that Miss Fowler and she had ever written to him, kept for some absurd reason through all these years; a five-day attempt at a diary; framed pictures of racing motors in full Brooklands career, and load upon load of undistinguishable wreckage of tool-boxes, rabbit-hutches, electric batteries, tin soldiers, fret-saw outfits, and jig-saw puzzles.

Miss Fowler at the window watched her come and go, and said to herself, 'Mary's an old woman. I never realised it before.'

After lunch she recommended her to rest.

'I'm not in the least tired,' said Mary. 'I've got it all arranged. I'm going to the village at two o'clock for some paraffin. Nellie hasn't enough, and the walk will do me good.'

She made one last quest round the house before she started, and found that she had overlooked nothing. It began to mist as soon as she had skirted Vegg's Heath, where Wynn used to descend—it seemed to her that she could almost hear the beat of his propellers overhead, but there was nothing to see. She hoisted her umbrella and lunged into the blind wet till she had reached the shelter of the empty village. As she came out of Mr. Kidd's shop with a bottle full of paraffin in her string shopping-bag, she met Nurse Eden, the village nurse, and fell into talk with her, as usual, about the village children. They were just parting opposite the 'Royal Oak,' when a gun, they fancied, was fired immediately behind the house. It was followed by a child's shriek dying into a wail.

'Accident!' said Nurse Eden promptly, and dashed through the empty bar, followed by Mary. They found Mrs. Gerritt, the publican's wife, who could only gasp and point to the yard, where a little cart-lodge was sliding sideways amid a clatter of tiles. Nurse Eden snatched up a sheet drying before the fire, ran out, lifted something from the ground, and flung the sheet round it. The sheet turned scarlet and half her uniform too, as she bore the load into the kitchen. It was little Edna Gerritt, aged nine, whom Mary had known since her perambulator days.

'Am I hurted bad?' Edna asked, and died between Nurse Eden's dripping hands. The sheet fell aside, and for an instant, before she could shut her eyes, Mary saw the ripped and shredded body.

'It's a wonder she spoke at all,' said Nurse Eden. 'What in God's name was it?'

'A bomb,' said Mary.

'One o' the Zeppelins?'

'No. An aeroplane. I thought I heard it on the Heath, but I fancied it was one of ours. It must have shut off its engines as it came down. That's why we didn't notice it.'

'The filthy pigs!' said Nurse Eden, all white and shaken. 'See the pickle I'm in! Go and tell Dr. Hennis, Miss Postgate.' Nurse looked at the mother, who had dropped face down on the floor. 'She's only in a fit. Turn her over.'

Mary heaved Mrs. Gerritt right side up, and hurried off for the doctor. When she told her tale, he asked her to sit down in the surgery till he got her something.

'But I don't need it, I assure you,' said she. 'I don't think it would be wise to tell Miss Fowler about it, do you? Her heart is so irritable in this weather.'

Dr. Hennis looked at her admiringly as he packed up his bag.

'No. Don't tell anybody till we're sure,' he said, and hastened to the 'Royal Oak,' while Mary went on with the paraffin. The village behind her was as quiet as usual, for the news had not yet spread. She frowned a little to herself, her large nostrils expanded uglily, and from time to time she muttered a phrase which Wynn, who never restrained himself before his women-folk, had applied to the enemy. 'Bloody pagans! They *are* bloody pagans. But,' she continued, falling back on the teaching that had made her what she was, 'one mustn't let one's mind dwell on these things.'

Before she reached the house Dr. Hennis, who was also a special constable, overtook her in his car.

'Oh, Miss Postgate,' he said, 'I wanted to tell you that that accident at the "Royal Oak" was due to Gerritt's stable tumbling down. It's been dangerous for a long time. It ought to have been condemned.'

'I thought I heard an explosion too,' said Mary.

'You might have been misled by the beams snapping. I've been looking at 'em. They were dry-rotted through and through. Of course, as they broke, they would make a noise just like a gun.'

'Yes?' said Mary politely.

'Poor little Edna was playing underneath it,' he went on, still holding her with his eyes, 'and that and the tiles cut her to pieces, you see?'

'I saw it,' said Mary, shaking her head. 'I heard it too.'

'Well, we cannot be sure.' Dr. Hennis changed his tone completely. 'I know both you and Nurse Eden (I've been speaking to her) are perfectly trustworthy, and I can rely on you not to say anything—yet, at least. It is no good to stir up people unless—'

'Oh, I never do—anyhow,' said Mary, and Dr. Hennis went on to the county town.

After all, she told herself, it might, just possibly, have been the collapse of the old stable that had done all those things to poor little Edna. She was sorry she had even hinted at other things, but Nurse Eden was discretion itself. By the time she reached home the affair seemed increasingly remote by its very monstrosity. As she came in, Miss Fowler told her that a couple of aeroplanes had passed half an hour ago.

'I thought I heard them,' she replied. 'I'm going down to the garden now. I've got the paraffin.'

'Yes, but—what *have* you got on your boots? They're soaking wet. Change them at once.'

Not only did Mary obey, but she wrapped the boots in a newspaper and put them into the string bag with the bottle. So, armed with the longest kitchen poker, she left.

'It's raining again,' was Miss Fowler's last word, 'but—I know you won't be happy till that's disposed of.'

'It won't take long. I've got everything down there, and I've put the lid on the destructor to keep the wet out.'

The shrubbery was filling with twilight by the time she had completed her arrangements and sprinkled the sacrificial oil. As she lit the match that would burn her heart to ashes, she heard a groan or a grunt behind the dense Portugal laurels.

'Cheape?' she called impatiently, but Cheape, with his ancient lumbago, in his comfortable cottage, would be the last man to profane the sanctuary. 'Sheep,' she concluded, and threw in the fusee. The pyre went up in a roar, and the immediate flame hastened night around her.

'How Wynn would have loved this!' she thought, stepping back from the blaze.

By its light she saw, half hidden behind a laurel not five paces away, a bareheaded man sitting very stiffly at the foot of one of the oaks. A broken branch lay across his lap—one booted leg protruding from beneath it. His head moved ceaselessly from side to side, but his body was as still as the tree's trunk. He was dressed—she moved sideways to look more closely—in a uniform something like Wynn's, with a flap buttoned across the chest. For an instant, she had some idea that it might be one of the young flying men she had met at the funeral. But their heads were dark and glossy. This man's was as pale as a baby's, and so closely cropped that she could see the disgusting pinky skin beneath. His lips moved.

'What do you say?' Mary moved towards him and stooped.

'Laty! Laty! Laty!' he muttered, while his hands picked at the dead wet leaves. There was no doubt as to his nationality. It made her so angry that she strode back to the destructor, though it was still too hot to use the poker there. Wynn's books seemed to be catching well. She looked up at the oak behind the man; several of the light upper and two or three rotten lower branches had broken and scattered their rubbish on the shrubbery path. On the lowest fork a helmet with dependent strings showed like a bird's-nest in the light of a long-tongued flame. Evidently this person had fallen through the tree. Wynn had told her that it was quite possible for people to fall out of aeroplanes. Wynn had told her, too, that trees were useful things to break an aviator's fall, but in this case the aviator must have been broken or he would have moved from his queer position. He seemed helpless except for his horrible rolling head. On the other hand, she could see a pistol case at his belt—and Mary loathed pistols. Months ago, after reading certain Belgian reports together, she and Miss Fowler had had dealings with one—a huge revolver with flat-nosed bullets, which latter, Wynn said, were forbidden by the rules of war to be used against civilised enemies. 'They're good enough for us,' Miss Fowler had replied. 'Show Mary how it works.' And Wynn, laughing at the mere possibility of any such need, had led the craven winking Mary into the Rector's disused quarry, and had shown her how to fire the terrible machine. It lay now in the top-left-hand drawer of her toilet-table—a memento not included in the burning. Wynn would be pleased to see how she was not afraid.

She slipped up to the house to get it. When she came through the rain, the eyes in the head were alive with expectation. The mouth even tried to smile. But at sight of the revolver its corners went down just like Edna Gerritt's. A tear trickled from one eye, and the head rolled from shoulder to shoulder as though trying to point out something.

'Cassée. Tout cassée,' it whimpered.

'What do you say?' said Mary disgustedly, keeping well to one side, though only the head moved.

'Cassée,' it repeated. 'Che me rends. Le médicin! Toctor!'

'Nein!' said she, bringing all her small German to bear with the big pistol. 'Ich haben der todt Kinder gesehen.'

The head was still. Mary's hand dropped. She had been careful to keep her finger off the trigger for fear of accidents. After a few moments' waiting, she returned to the destructor, where the flames were falling, and churned up Wynn's charring books with the poker. Again the head groaned for the doctor.

'Stop that!' said Mary, and stamped her foot. 'Stop that, you bloody pagan!'

The words came quite smoothly and naturally. They were Wynn's own words, and Wynn was a gentleman who for no consideration on earth would have torn little Edna into those vividly coloured strips and strings. But this thing hunched under the oak-tree had done that thing. It was no question of reading horrors out of newspapers to Miss Fowler. Mary had seen it with her own eyes on the 'Royal Oak' kitchen table. She must not allow her mind to dwell upon it. Now Wynn was dead, and everything connected with him was lumping and rustling and tinkling under her busy poker into red black dust and grey leaves of ash. The thing beneath the oak would die too. Mary had seen death more than once. She came of a family that had a knack of dying under, as she told Miss Fowler, 'most distressing circumstances.' She would stay where she was till she was entirely satisfied that It was dead—dead as dear papa in the late 'eighties; aunt Mary in 'eighty-nine; mamma in 'ninety-one; cousin Dick in 'ninety-five; Lady McCausland's housemaid in 'ninety-nine; Lady McCausland's sister in nineteen hundred and one; Wynn buried five days ago; and Edna Gerritt still waiting for decent earth to hide her. As she thought—her underlip caught up by one faded canine, brows knit and nostrils wide—she wielded the poker with lunges that jarred the grating at the bottom, and careful scrapes round the brick-work above. She looked at her wrist-watch. It was getting on to half-past four, and the rain was coming down in earnest. Tea would be at five. If It did not die before that time, she would be soaked and would have to change. Meantime, and this occupied her, Wynn's things were burning well in spite of the hissing wet, though now and again a book-back with a quite distinguishable title would be heaved up out of the mass. The exercise of stoking had given her a glow which seemed to reach to the marrow of her bones. She hummed—Mary never had a voice—to herself. She had never believed in all those advanced views—though Miss Fowler herself leaned a little that way—of woman's work in the world; but now she saw there was much to be said for them. This, for instance, was *her* work—work which no man, least of all Dr. Hennis, would ever have done. A man, at such a crisis, would be what Wynn called a 'sportsman'; would leave everything to fetch help, and would certainly bring It into the house. Now a woman's business was to make a happy home for—for a husband and children. Failing these—it was not a thing one should allow one's mind to dwell upon—but——

'Stop it!' Mary cried once more across the shadows. 'Nein, I tell you! Ich haben der todt Kinder gesehen.'

But it was a fact. A woman who had missed these things could still be useful—more useful than a man in certain respects. She thumped like a pavior through the settling ashes at the secret thrill of it. The rain was damping the fire, but she could feel—it was too dark to see—that her work was done. There was a dull red glow at the bottom of the destructor, not enough to char the wooden lid if she slipped it half over against the driving wet. This arranged, she leaned on the poker and waited, while an increasing rapture laid hold on her. She ceased to think. She gave herself up to feel. Her long pleasure was broken by a sound that she had waited for in agony several times in her life. She leaned forward and listened, smiling. There could be no mistake. She closed her eyes and drank it in. Once it ceased abruptly.

'Go on,' she murmured, half aloud. 'That isn't the end.'

Then the end came very distinctly in a lull between two rain-gusts. Mary Postgate drew her breath short between her teeth and shivered from head to foot. *'That's* all right,' said she contentedly, and went up to the house, where she scandalised the whole routine by taking a luxurious hot bath before tea, and came down looking, as Miss Fowler said when she saw her lying all relaxed on the other sofa, 'quite handsome!'

The Wolf
by Guy de Maupassant

Here is what the old Marquis d'Arville told us towards the end of St. Hubert's dinner at the house of the Baron des Ravels.

We had killed a stag that day. The marquis was the only one of the guests who had not taken any part in this chase, for he never hunted.

All through that long repast we had talked about hardly anything but the slaughter of animals. The ladies themselves were interested in tales sanguinary and often unlikely, and the orators imitated the attacks and the combats of men against beasts, raised their arms, romanced in a thundering voice.

M. d'Arville talked well, with a certain poetry of style somewhat high-sounding, but full of effect. He must have repeated this story often, for he told it fluently, not hesitating on words, choosing them with skill to produce a picture—

Gentlemen, I have never hunted; neither did my father, nor my grandfather, nor my great-grandfather. This last was the son of a man who hunted more than all of you put together. He died in 1764. I will tell you how.

His name was Jean. He was married, father of that child who became my ancestor, and he lived with his younger brother, François d'Arville, in our castle in Lorraine, in the middle of the forest.

François d'Arville had remained a bachelor for love of the chase.

They both hunted from one end of the year to the other, without repose, without stopping, without fatigue. They loved only that, understood nothing else, talked only of that, lived only for that.

They had at heart that one passion, which was terrible and inexorable. It consumed them, having entirely invaded them, leaving place for no other.

They had given orders that they should not be interrupted in the chase, for any reason whatever. My great-grandfather was born while his father was following a fox, and Jean d'Arville did not stop his pursuit, but he swore: "Name of a name, that rascal there might have waited till after the view-halloo!"

His brother François showed himself still more infatuated. On rising he went to see the dogs, then the horses; then he shot little birds about the castle until the moment for departing to hunt down some great beast.

In the country-side they were called M. le Marquis and M. le Cadet, the nobles then not doing at all like the chance nobility of our time, which wishes to establish an hereditary hierarchy in titles; for the son of a marquis is no more a count, nor the son of a viscount a baron, than the son of a general is a colonel by birth. But the mean vanity of to-day finds profit in that arrangement.

I return to my ancestors.

They were, it seems, immeasurably tall, bony, hairy, violent, and vigorous. The younger, still taller than the older, had a voice so strong that, according to a legend of which he was proud, all the leaves of the forests shook when he shouted.

And when they both mounted to go off to the hunt, that must have been a superb spectacle to see those two giants straddling their huge horses.

Now towards the midwinter of that year, 1764, the frosts were excessive, and the wolves became ferocious.

They even attacked belated peasants, roamed at night about the houses, howled from sunset to sunrise, and de-populated the stables.

And soon a rumor began to circulate. People talked of a colossal wolf, with gray fur, almost white, who had eaten two children, gnawed off a woman's arm, strangled all the dogs of the *garde du pays*, and penetrated without fear into the farm-yards to come snuffling under the doors. The people in the houses affirmed that they had felt his breath, and that it made the flame of the lights flicker. And soon a panic ran through all the province. No one dared go out any more after night-fall. The shades seemed haunted by the image of the beast.

The brothers d'Arville resolved to find and kill him, and several times they assembled all the gentlemen of the country to a great hunting.

In vain. They might beat the forest and search the coverts; they never met him. They killed wolves, but not that one. And every night after a *battue*, the beast, as if to avenge himself, attacked some traveller or devoured someone's cattle, always far from the place where they had looked for him.

Finally one night he penetrated into the pig-pen of the Château d'Arville and ate the two finest pigs.

The brothers were inflamed with anger, considering this attack as a bravado of the monster, an insult direct, a defiance. They took their strong blood-hounds used to pursue formidable beasts, and they set off to hunt, their hearts swollen with fury.

From dawn until the hour when the empurpled sun descended behind the great naked trees, they beat the thickets without finding anything.

At last, furious and disconsolate, both were returning, walking their horses along an *allée* bordered with brambles, and they marvelled that their woodcraft should be crossed so by this wolf, and they were seized suddenly with a sort of mysterious fear.

The elder said:

"That beast there is not an ordinary one. You would say it thought like a man."

The younger answered:

"Perhaps we should have a bullet blessed by our cousin, the bishop, or pray some priest to pronounce the words which are needed."

Then they were silent.

Jean continued:

"Look how red the sun is. The great wolf will do some harm to-night."

He had hardly finished speaking when his horse reared; that of François began to kick. A large thicket covered with dead leaves opened before them, and a colossal beast, quite gray, sprang up and ran off across the wood.

Both uttered a kind of groan of joy, and, bending over the necks of their heavy horses, they threw them forward with an impulse from their whole bodies, hurling them on at such a pace, exciting them, hurrying them away, maddening them so with the voice, with gesture, and with spur that the strong riders seemed rather to be carrying the heavy beasts between their thighs and to bear them off as if they were flying.

Thus they went, *ventre à terre*, bursting the thickets, cleaving the beds of streams, climbing the hill-sides, descending the gorges, and blowing on the horn with full lungs to attract their people and their dogs.

And now, suddenly, in that mad race, my ancestor struck his forehead against an enormous branch which split his skull; and he fell stark dead on the ground, while his frightened horse took himself off, disappearing in the shade which enveloped the woods.

The cadet of Arville stopped short, leaped to the earth, and seized his brother in his arms. He saw that the brains ran from the wound with the blood.

Then he sat down beside the body, rested the head, disfigured and red, on his knees, and waited, contemplating that immobile face of the elder brother. Little by little a fear invaded him, a strange fear which he had never felt before, the fear of the dark, the fear of solitude, the fear of the deserted wood, and the fear also of the fantastic wolf who had just killed his brother to avenge himself upon them both.

The shadows thickened; the acute cold made the trees crack. François got up, shivering, unable to remain there longer, feeling himself almost growing faint. Nothing was to be heard, neither the voice of the dogs nor the sound of the horns—all was silent along the invisible horizon; and this mournful silence of the frozen night had something about it frightening and strange.

He seized in his colossal hands the great body of Jean, straightened it and laid it across the saddle to carry it back to the château; then he went on his way softly, his mind troubled as if he were drunken, pursued by horrible and surprising images.

And abruptly, in the path which the night was invading, a great shape passed. It was the beast. A shock of terror shook the hunter; something cold, like a drop of water, glided along his veins, and, like a monk haunted of the devil, he made a great sign of the cross, dismayed at this abrupt return of the frightful prowler. But his eyes fell back upon the inert body laid before him, and suddenly, passing abruptly from fear to anger, he shook with an inordinate rage.

Then he spurred his horse and rushed after the wolf.

He followed it by the copses, the ravines, and the tall trees, traversing woods which he no longer knew, his eyes fixed on the white speck which fled before him through the night now fallen upon the earth.

His horse also seemed animated by a force and an ardor hitherto unknown. It galloped, with outstretched neck, straight on, hurling against the trees, against the rocks, the head and the feet of the dead man thrown across the saddle. The briers tore out the hair; the brow, beating the huge trunks, spattered them with blood; the spurs tore their ragged coats of bark. And suddenly the beast and the horseman issued from the forest and rushed into a valley, just as the moon appeared above the mountains. This valley was stony, closed by enormous rocks, without possible issue; and the wolf was cornered and turned round.

François then uttered a yell of joy which the echoes repeated like a rolling of thunder, and he leaped from his horse, his cutlass in his hand.

The beast, with bristling hair, the back arched, awaited him; its eyes glistened like two stars. But, before offering battle, the strong hunter, seizing his brother, seated him on a rock, and, supporting with stones his head, which was no more than a blot of blood, he shouted in the ears as if he was talking to a deaf man, "Look, Jean; look at this!"

Then he threw himself upon the monster. He felt himself strong enough to overturn a mountain, to bruise stones in his hands. The beast tried to bite him, seeking to strike in at his stomach; but he had seized it by the neck, without even using his weapon, and he strangled it gently, listening to the stoppage of the breathings in its throat and the beatings of its heart. And he laughed, rejoicing madly, pressing closer and closer his formidable embrace, crying in a delirium of joy, "Look, Jean, look!" All resistance ceased; the body of the wolf became lax. He was dead.

Then François, taking him up in his arms, carried him off and went and threw him at the feet of the elder brother, repeating, in a tender voice, "There, there, there, my little Jean, see him!"

Then he replaced on the saddle the two bodies one upon the other; and he went his way.

He returned to the château, laughing and crying, like Gargantua at the birth of Pantagruel, uttering shouts of triumph and stamping with joy in relating the death of the beast, and moaning and tearing his beard in telling that of his brother.

And often, later, when he talked again of that day, he said, with tears in his eyes, "If only that poor Jean could have seen me strangle the other, he would have died content. I am sure of it!"

The widow of my ancestor inspired her orphan son with that horror of the chase which has transmitted itself from father to son as far down as myself.

The Marquis d'Arville was silent. Someone asked:

"That story is a legend, isn't it?"

And the story-teller answered:

"I swear to you that it is true from one end to the other."

Then a lady declared, in a little, soft voice:

"All the same, it is fine to have passions like that."

A Duel by Candlelight
by Andreas Latzko

The baronial castle of Gyoroky, in Transylvania, was destroyed at the end of the fifteenth century by a passing horde of Turks. For centuries its moss-grown ruins had no other inhabitants than a few emaciated goats, and the descendants of the lords of Gyoroky, who in the days of old had plundered every convoy of merchandise that passed near their stronghold, and were now but a modest family of Austrian officers.

Within the memory of these survivors, no Baron Gyoroky had known what it was to eat and drink to his heart's content; all were giants in limb and muscle, but their portion of the good things of life was no more than that of ordinary men. Reduced circumstances had tamed their spirit, and the feudal brigands of yore passed from the severe routine of the Cadets' school to the barrack-square, where they were limited to bullying young recruits.

At last rescue came.

A little German professor of geology visited Gyoroky on holiday. His idea had been to hunt for traces of Saxon elements there, tossed by a historic tempest as far as Transylvania. Instead, he went up hill and down dale, tapping with his little hammer all the bits of rock he found, sounding

them like a physician. Finally he carried off two sacks full of
stones.

To the general surprise, he returned some months later,
accompanied by an imposing procession of motor cars.

Included in this escort was the last scion of the house of
Gyoroky. Laced into the uniform of an infantry officer, the
lieutenant sulkily strode into the smoky parlor of the village
inn, openly distrustful of the mad professor and the whole
company of financiers and lawyers. He sat inattentively
through a tedious discussion, supporting himself with copi-
ous draughts of the familiar sour wine of the district. The
wine and the monotonous murmur of the speeches, which
conveyed nothing at all to him, made him so sleepy that he
thought he was dreaming in good earnest when he heard his
own name, and found himself appointed chairman.

His distrust increased as he looked at the imposing
document which he was asked to sign in connection with the
issue of shares numbered 1 to 100,000. The lieutenant's
experience of papers with large figures above and his signature below had not been happy. And the unencumbered
portion of his meagre pay did not admit of any further
signatures.

In vain did the others try to explain to the officer the
difference between a promissory note and a share; a baron of
Gyoroky was above these Jewish subtleties, and he was on
the point of exploding when the magic word "advance"
promptly dissipated both his annoyance and the effects of
the wine. After much hesitation, scared at his own effron-
tery, and mainly in order to get rid of the fellows, he asked
for 10,000 Austrian crowns—say £400. When no one de-
murred he was confirmed in his suspicion, and when he
placed ten irreproachable 1000-crown notes in his worn
pocket-book he felt sure that he was dealing with a band of
brigands. Anyhow, for once he had got some money out of
the Jews without any prospect of its return. For it would have

been quite impossible to produce ten thousand crowns out of what was still assignable of his pay, even though he lived to the age of Methuselah. That was the end of that.

He soon learned better. The counterfoils of his check-book taught the chairman of the new mining company the value of his signature. Instead of reducing the worth of the paper on which he placed it, as had happened sometimes in the past, his scrawl now transformed every sheet into money. The lord of Gyoroky was not a man to disdain this magic power. On the contrary, the vague fear of seeing the beautiful dream end in a painful awakening urged him to put his power to the test. He indulged his most extravagant desires—and still the enchantment lasted.

Then the ancestral itch for authority, so long repressed, awoke in its primitive force. The feudal pride, humiliated for centuries, welled up, bursting the frail barrier of the codes of what is called civilization. Rich and powerful, Baron Gyoroky saw no reason for repressing his natural instincts. What if he had been born some centuries too late? He resumed the life of the lords of Gyoroky at the point at which his ancestors had had to abandon it.

From the open flanks of the old mountain there flowed inexhaustible dividends. On a neighboring summit the ancient fortress rose again, exact at all points to the descriptions and engravings of the family chronicle, with its wide moat filled with water, its drawbridge and its keep. But instead of the ancient bombards, long-range guns of the most modern type showed their muzzles, and machine guns lurked behind the ramparts. The garrison, however, wore the livery of the house of Gyoroky, and, before the gates, men-at-arms mounted guard with halberds, though the men thus attired were the best non-commissioned officers in the country, picked by the experienced baron from among his former subordinates.

With this bodyguard, his fortress, and his riches, the baron was a power in the State. He requisitioned what he fancied, and imprisoned anyone who disobeyed him. A person who was simpleton enough to try to prosecute him received from the authorities a reply to this effect: "Let the plaintiff himself serve the writ on the lord of the manor, and justice will take its course!" In fact, since the baron, putting threats into effect, had received writ-servers with machine-gun fire, there was no longer a magistrate sitting in Transylvania within range of New Gyoroky.

In the capital, the extravagances of the brigand baron were treated with amused indulgence. He became the hero of musical comedies. Picture-postcard factories and illustrated papers sent their photographers to Gyoroky, the latest arrival in the news. A reporter succeeded in getting engaged as a man-at-arms, and his description of the life of the castle was "splashed" in every popular newspaper in the whole world.

In time, however, the authorities began to tire of the complaints of the baron's behavior. The joke had lasted long enough, and it was decided, in principle, to put an end to it. In practice, there was hesitation in mobilizing the forces of the State against a single citizen; it might excite ridicule abroad. Even when the baron virtually invested the churches and carried off such brides as he fancied, on the strength of the *jus primae noctis* of his ancestors, it was preferred to turn a blind eye to his excesses, and the scandal was hushed up. Indiscreet journalists were taken to task for publishing objectionable reports, but the ogre was able to keep the young brides captive in his fortress, without fear of justice or of the vengeance of the outraged husbands. The wisest of these made no boast of their predicament, and thus avoided adding mockery to misfortune.

However, the urgency of the prelates at last persuaded the

State to act. A lien was placed on all the bank accounts of the lord of Gyoroky, and he was threatened with the blockade of his castle. The baron replied by levelling all his guns at the neighboring mine-workings, threatening to reduce to atoms the property of his fellow shareholders unless they did something to protect him from the attacks of the Church.

In this fight between big capital and the high clergy, it was the worldly power that won. The severest sanctions were discussed, but once more the affair was allowed to drop, since a few injured husbands could not outweigh the social significance of an enterprise capitalized at millions. The public was informed that in view of the necessity of protecting the miners' families from the disaster of unemployment, nothing more could be done.

So the laugh was once more on the baron's side, and the only practical result of this affair of state was to demonstrate to the lord of Gyoroky the necessity of insuring against the danger of a siege. The national canning factories received an order on a scale that startled them.

After this decisive victory, the baron threw off all restraint. There was a regular *sauve qui peut* in the neighborhood; officials who had pretty wives asked to be transferred, landowners sold their estates at a loss; no sacrifice was too great to make for escape from the neighborhood of the lion's den. Those who were unavoidably retained in the vicinity of New Gyoroky made the best of a bad job, and discreetly went away on an alleged business journey when it came to the turn of their wives to make a more or less prolonged stay in the sumptuous private apartments of the castle. The reign of the Iron King was absolute. Villagers far around hid when, by the light of torches and to the beat of drums, the garrison of New Gyoroky passed by. The police set a good example, as was their duty; at the first sound of a raiding party they became completely invisible.

One day, when riding at no great distance from the castle, the baron discovered a delicious little person, with hair like a raven's wing; a surprising spectacle, as he supposed all this district to have been long exhausted. Inquiries revealed a simple explanation: the young woman with the dark eyes was the wife of Rabbi Samuel Levi, and the baron, now that he had money, had given up all intercourse with Jews. But Mrs. Levi was different. Here was an amorous domain beyond his ken. He embarked excitedly upon the exotic adventure.

Rabbi Samuel Levi was a delicate little man, with a thin pointed beard and twinkling eyes. His co-religionists considered him the cutest of them all. He noticed the baron's frequent torchlight rides past his house, and he was not wholly unprepared when one night, on his return home from officiating in a neighboring village, he found the nest empty. The flowers in the garden had been trampled by horses' hooves, the walls of his house blackened by torches; the furniture was in disorder as if there had been a raid, and the weeping servant related the unheard-of brutality with which her poor mistress had been carried off. But Samuel Levi glanced at the open wardrobe. He saw that the finest dresses and the best linen had vanished, and the gap helped him to bear his loss with manly composure.

Pronouncing the prescribed ritual curse against the "seduced" wife, he put on his silk cap and set off at once along the road to the fortress. Trotting as fast as his short legs would carry him, and murmuring his prayers as he went, he was barely two hours in reaching the castle. But he found the drawbridge raised and the gates barred. In answer to his shouts, the laughing guards, with mocking courtesy, begged him to be good enough to wait a little: the baron was too pleasantly occupied just then to receive visitors.

The rabbi nodded to signify that he quite understood. He

sat down on a moss-covered slab, opened his prayer book, and waited patiently. At last, toward sunset, the drawbridge was lowered with a thunderous rattling, the massive gates slowly opened, and a halberdier actually approached him and bade him welcome in the name of his master.

Little Samuel Levi, deaf to the tittering around him, gravely entered the imposing vault.

The lord of Gyoroky received the little man in the huge ancestral hall, his enormous body stretched in a gigantic armchair; from the magnificently chased golden cup that stood before him was wafted the aroma of a very old Tokay. He was in an excellent humor.

"And what can I do for you, Mr. Levi?" he asked patronizingly.

The rabbi bowed humbly, rubbed the palms of his hands together, and, after a moment's hesitation, declared with firmness:

"I have come to demand reparation from you, My Lord."

The baron jumped out of his chair in astonishment. Then he burst into a roar of laughter, and, producing his pocketbook, enquired:

"How much do you want, Mr. Levi?"

The shrewd eyes flashed for a moment. But the rabbi recovered his imperturbability. He replied, with due respect:

"Your lordship is pleased to jest. I know how fastidious are the lords of Gyoroky on a point of honor. You will not refuse me due reparation."

The baron's mouthful of Tokay nearly choked him. But with an effort he checked his laughter. He bowed low and replied:

"Very well, then! We will fight, little rabbi. I leave you the choice of weapons. It is for you, the injured party, to dictate the conditions of the duel. I undertake to respect them. As you see, there are rapiers and yataghans on the walls here.

Perhaps you prefer the heavy cavalry saber. There are plenty in my armory, with a first-class edge on them. Or pistols, rifles, guns, mortars—anything you like."

Samuel Levi raised his thin hands in a gesture of refusal.

"Why all this profusion, My Lord? You know well enough that I have no skill in the use of your lethal weapons. I have not come to challenge you in order to give myself up to be helplessly slaughtered. If you intend to give me satisfaction, you must leave it to me to state the conditions."

The baron bowed to the ground.

"And your conditions are—?" he asked.

The rabbi took two or three little steps forward.

"In the first place, your lordship will be so kind as to have yourself firmly tied to that armchair with stout ropes."

"Tied? I—tied?" cried the baron indignantly. "Not I!"

Levi made a hurried deprecating gesture.

"Pardon, pardon, My Lord, I shall merely see that it has been properly done, and then I will have myself similarly tied in this other chair. Your lordship can trust your men to make sure that they will bind me no less securely."

"What is the game?" said the baron, grudgingly giving way. "Let myself be bound! Get that out of your head, Jew!"

The rabbi spoke up with decision:

"Your lordship has yourself said that it is for me, as the injured party, to determine the conditions of the duel. Nobody will seriously suggest that a baron of Gyoroky would decline to keep his word. As I said, your servants will bind me with equally strong ropes. Just look at my arm, and you will agree that the condition cannot be prejudicial to you. Is it conceivable that a bound Jew should cause more fear to a baron of Gyoroky than *vice versa?*"

The baron flushed.

"Fear is a Hebrew word, Mr. Levi; excuse me for not understanding that language."

"Quite so! So there we are," said the rabbi, with satisfaction. "I am forced to insist on this condition, because I hope to wound you, My Lord, and you have a way of hitting out if one comes too close——"

"Faint heart!" laughed the baron. "If I fight with you, you are free to wound me as much as you can. But in your own interest, little man, I advise you to do without ropes. How can you talk with your hands tied? I give you my word of honor that, even without ropes, I will keep entirely to your conditions, and my word protects you better than the most powerful hawsers could."

"Surely, surely, My Lord! I know that is so, but you are reckoning without a force stronger than any word of honor, the force of habit. You would regret it, of course—you would be ready to cut off the arm that had made you break your word. But that would not help me. Unless I am mistaken, the windows of this hall look out over the great moat, with deep water in it——"

The baron burst out laughing:

"That's so. The windows are a hundred feet and more above the moat; you have the bump of locality, old chap. Well, now, this is a good joke. I'll agree to deliver myself to you bound hand and foot. I make only one condition: our duel must not last too long. No doubt you know there is better fun awaiting me than a *tête à tête* with a trussed Jew!"

Nothing in the rabbi's bony face revealed that he understood the allusion. The baron put a heavy hand on his shoulder and gave him a confiding wink:

"You will allow me, Mr. Levi, to drink one more cup of Tokay, to give me courage before the duel. Perhaps you too will accept a cup?"

"I thank you, My Lord; but I prefer water. Will you, however, do me the honor of drinking both glasses?"

"With the greatest of pleasure, good rabbi. While I am about it, give your orders. I don't think we shall need a surgeon under your prudent system of trussed duellists?"

The rabbi discreetly left this question unanswered, only smiling faintly with satisfaction as the lord of the manor had his enormous goblet filled twice to the brim, and swallowed the heavy Tokay like so much water. After that, Samuel Levi carefully superintended the work of the servants. The baron's arms were securely bound with three turns of rope to the arms of his chair, and his whole body, from chest to ankles, to the back, seat, and legs of the heavy piece of oak furniture. Levi tested the ropes, found here and there a knot insufficiently tight—and finally sat down exactly three paces away, opposite the baron, and was bound with equally strong ropes to a similar armchair. He himself warned the servants to draw the bonds round his skinny arms no less tightly than round the bulging muscles of their master's. Everything must be done with rigorous correctness. He fully appreciated the honor of measuring himself against a Baron Gyoroky!

Lastly, fresh candles were placed in the great candelabra, and, at the request of the rabbi, the baron formally prohibited anyone from entering the hall until daybreak, whatever noise might be heard. The servants obediently withdrew, the doors were closed, the footsteps died away; the duellers were alone.

Then an extraordinary thing happened.

The mighty lord of New Gyoroky, who had never before known fear, had the impression of being suddenly crippled and cast upon a desert island, abandoned by the whole world, and struck off the roll of living men. The slight spluttering of the candles in the deep silence called up memories of a night spent on guard at a lying-in-state; the enforced immobility, the loss of power over his muscles, suggested the immobility of the corpse in its coffin. A cold shiver ran down the baron's spine.

He pulled himself together and looked across with a

mocking smile at the little Jew, prepared to laugh at his ridiculous appearance.

But the sight of the little man sitting trussed up opposite to him froze his blood, just as if he had seen Satan himself in the chair.

Every trace of inferiority, every sign of respect had vanished from Samuel Levi's face. A disquieting and inexorable assurance shone from his little eyes, while his glance measured the powerful frame of this baron of Gyoroky. He looked as sure of victory as a practised duellist about to use his deadliest thrust to transfix his adversary.

The baron was very near calling for his servants.

"Come, come, little man!" he burst out, chaffingly, but grimacing as though every word had to be dragged from his mouth like a tooth. "I feel very like going to sleep, and then all the guns in the castle could not wake me. So hurry up with your 'wounding.' "

"I'm just going to!" replied the rabbi cheerfully, and his face showed how much at ease he felt in his bonds. At the first considered words that he spoke, the last traces of uncertainty disappeared, and he seemed like a man set free.

"So, you have—as your friends would put it—seduced my wife, and you are very proud of your success? I wonder why. If I were a Baron Gyoroky I should have begun by looking for a pretty young maid, and only afterwards, when I was tired of her, should I have married her to Rabbi Levi. For Rabbi Levi that, I must say, would have been a bitter pill. But, thank goodness, you are content to have it the other way round. You say 'After you, Mr. Levi!' Well, I reply 'With pleasure!' If you are so modest as to take my leavings, it is a matter of taste. You may keep your bit of fluff."

The baron smiled sourly:

"Thank you, rabbi. It is not a bad bit of fluff; the only thing is to know how to get hold of it."

Samuel Levi bowed approvingly:

"Quite so, My Lord, quite so. We others go and find ourselves wives, young and virgin, in their parents' homes, without serenading or seduction nonsense. It is only then that your sort comes along, with your flowers and chocolates, even jewellery, and set out to conquer women who are deflowered and out of currency. It mystifies me. Is it your modesty or your stupidity?"

The baron paled:

"None of your insolence, Jew! Don't forget that my word of honor protects you only until dawn!"

"Are you hurt already?" said the rabbi. "I thought I was free to do my worst to wound you. Are you straining at your bonds so soon? It seems as if you are the one that needs his hands to talk with."

"Cowardly dog!" growled the baron. "How you would beg for mercy if only I had my right arm free!"

Samuel Levi's face shone. His voice grew hard and grating. He hacked at his adversary as though with the beak of a vulture:

"Why do you call me coward? Am I not tied to my chair just like you, and telling you the truth to your face? Is that cowardly? As for cowardice, what of yourself? As far back as your family chronicle goes, no Gyoroky has ever refrained from insulting and beating men who were defenceless, men in chains. Did you not torment your soldiers because discipline forbade them to retaliate? You—Gyorokys—did you not whip your serfs, and rob your merchants? Did you not squander their substance in drinking dens and gaming hells, always yourselves armed and surrounded by armed men, armed against trembling and helpless victims? That is the sort of cowardly dogs your ancestors were—and you yourself—"

"Another word about my ancestors, and I will kill you, Jew!" roared the baron in his fury.

"When?" laughed the rabbi contemptuously. "Tomorrow

morning, perhaps? I can believe it. Tomorrow morning, when I am once more the weak and defenceless little Jew, and you are lord of the manor of New Gyoroky, with all your men. But why are you helpless now, when we are equals? I am using no arms against you, I have no servants at my back, and yet here you are squirming and grinding your teeth like a caged gorilla. Do you see now what a miserable coward you are?"

The words died on the rabbi's paling lips, for Baron Gyoroky, with a terrific heave, brought his seat so far forward that the arms of the two chairs touched. Levi shrank back in mortal fear; he could feel the baron's panting breath on his face, as though his head were now in the jaws of a wild beast. In terrified fascination he watched the powerful arms twisting in their bonds, like harpooned sharks.

But the knots held.

The rabbi breathed again. He shouted into his adversary's purple face:

"You brute beast! I will suffocate you with your own rage!"

The baron managed to regain command of himself. Quietly, almost inaudibly, he whispered between his clenched teeth:

"I am sorry for you, Jew. You have no notion of what is in store for you in the morning!"

"Don't worry about me," Levi jeered. "Unless I greatly overestimate my powers, you will have a stroke before midnight."

"Murder! Help!" gasped the other. The affront was beyond bearing. This worm, this louse—and he could not move two fingers to smash it! Raving fury clutched at his throat, hammered at his temples, set the blood surging through his swelling veins. The giant whimpered like a child, quelled by the malevolently grinning face bent over his own.

"Well, who is the cowardly dog?" shouted the rabbi in his

ear. "Now do you know how good it is to be bound hand and foot? Can you feel what it means to be gagged and helpless? Wasn't it fine fun to chain men to a bench and whip them until they began to whimper like children? . . . Squeal away! You yourself, you fool, gave orders that nobody was to enter. I shall let you suffocate . . . trample on you . . . not a soldier, not a gun: on equal terms. Ha! You are blue already. Keep it up! . . ."

The baron made a supreme, superhuman effort to burst his bonds.

Then, suddenly, with a deafening crash, the back of the armchair broke in two, the arms came asunder, and the lord of the manor of Gyoroky was on his feet, with the pieces of the broken chair clinging to him like fragments of a shattered coat of mail.

Samuel Levi raised a piercing shriek to his God, and, with his head shrunk between his shoulders, waited for death.

But the blow did not fall. The baron swung round, made a few queer dance-like steps, clutched the air as if in search of a hold—and crumpled up, half buried under the heavy timbers of the broken chair.

Outside, the tower clock chimed the last quarter before midnight.

When, hours later, after vainly knocking and listening at the door, the servants at last ventured into the hall, they found the candles burnt down, and little Samuel Levi snoring loudly in his armchair, his weedy beard fluttering in the morning breeze.

At his feet the lord of Gyoroky, nicknamed the Iron King, lay stretched out, stone dead.

Roman Fever
by Edith Wharton

I

From the table at which they had been lunching two American ladies of ripe but well-cared-for middle age moved across the lofty terrace of the Roman restaurant and, leaning on its parapet, looked first at each other, and then down on the outspread glories of the Palatine and the Forum, with the same expression of vague but benevolent approval.

As they leaned there a girlish voice echoed up gaily from the stairs leading to the court below. "Well, come along, then," it cried, not to them but to an invisible companion, "and let's leave the young things to their knitting"; and a voice as fresh laughed back: "Oh, look here, Babs, not actually knitting—" "Well, I mean figuratively," rejoined the first. "After all, we haven't left our poor parents much else to do . . ." and at that point the turn of the stairs engulfed the dialogue.

The two ladies looked at each other again, this time with a tinge of smiling embarrassment, and the smaller and paler one shook her head and coloured slightly.

"Barbara!" she murmured, sending an unheard rebuke after the mocking voice in the stairway.

The other lady, who was fuller, and higher in colour, with a small determined nose supported by vigorous black eyebrows, gave a good-humoured laugh. "That's what our daughters think of us!"

Her companion replied by a deprecating gesture. "Not of us individually. We must remember that. It's just the collective modern idea of Mothers. And you see—" Half guiltily she drew from her handsomely mounted black hand-bag a twist of crimson silk run through by two fine knitting needles. "One never knows," she murmured. "The new system has certainly given us a good deal of time to kill; and sometimes I get tired just looking—even at this." Her gesture was now addressed to the stupendous scene at their feet.

The dark lady laughed again, and they both relapsed upon the view, contemplating it in silence, with a sort of diffused serenity which might have been borrowed from the spring effulgence of the Roman skies. The luncheon-hour was long past, and the two had their end of the vast terrace to themselves. At its opposite extremity a few groups, detained by a lingering look at the outspread city, were gathering up guide-books and fumbling for tips. The last of them scattered, and the two ladies were alone on the air-washed height.

"Well, I don't see why we shouldn't just stay here," said Mrs. Slade, the lady of the high colour and energetic brows. Two derelict basketchairs stood near, and she pushed them into the angle of the parapet and settled herself in one, her gaze upon the Palatine. "After all, it's still the most beautiful view in the world."

"It always will be, to me," assented her friend Mrs. Ansley, with so slight a stress on the "me" that Mrs. Slade, though she noticed it, wondered if it were not merely accidental, like the random underlinings of old-fashioned letter-writers.

"Grace Ansley was always old-fashioned," she thought; and added aloud, with a retrospective smile: "It's a view we've both been familiar with for a good many years. When we first met here we were younger than our girls are now. You remember?"

"Oh, yes, I remember," murmured Mrs. Ansley, with the same undefinable stress. "There's that head-waiter wondering," she interpolated. She was evidently far less sure than her companion of herself and of her rights in the world.

"I'll cure him of wondering," said Mrs. Slade, stretching her hand toward a bag as discreetly opulent-looking as Mrs. Ansley's. Signing to the head-waiter, she explained that she and her friend were old lovers of Rome and would like to spend the end of the afternoon looking down on the view—that is, if it did not disturb the service? The head-waiter, bowing over her gratuity, assured her that the ladies were most welcome, and would be still more so if they would condescend to remain for dinner. A full-moon night, they would remember . . .

Mrs. Slade's black brows drew together, as though references to the moon were out-of-place and even unwelcome. But she smiled away her frown as the head-waiter retreated. "Well, why not? We might do worse. There's no knowing, I suppose, when the girls will be back. Do you even know back from *where?* I don't!"

Mrs. Ansley again coloured slightly. "I think those young Italian aviators we met at the Embassy invited them to fly to Tarquinia for tea. I suppose they'll want to wait and fly back by moonlight."

"Moonlight—moonlight! What a part it still plays. Do you suppose they're as sentimental as we were?"

"I've come to the conclusion that I don't in the least know what they are," said Mrs. Ansley. "And perhaps we didn't know much more about each other."

"No; perhaps we didn't."

Her friend gave her a shy glance. "I never should have supposed you were sentimental, Alida."

"Well, perhaps I wasn't." Mrs. Slade drew her lids together in retrospect; and for a few moments the two ladies, who had been intimate since childhood, reflected how little they knew each other. Each one, of course, had a label ready to attach to the other's name; Mrs. Delphin Slade, for instance, would have told herself, or anyone who asked her, that Mrs. Horace Ansley, twenty-five years ago, had been exquisitely lovely—no, you wouldn't believe it, would you? . . . though, of course, still charming, distinguished . . . Well, as a girl she had been exquisite; far more beautiful than her daughter Barbara, though certainly Babs, according to the new standards at any rate, was more effective— had more *edge,* as they say. Funny where she got it, with those two nullities as parents. Yes; Horace Ansley was— well, just the duplicate of his wife. Museum specimens of old New York. Good-looking, irreproachable, exemplary. Mrs. Slade and Mrs. Ansley had lived opposite each other—actually as well as figuratively—for years. When the drawing-room curtains in No. 20 East 73rd Street were renewed, No. 23, across the way, was always aware of it. And of all the movings, buyings, travels, anniversaries, illnesses—the tame chronicle of an estimable pair. Little of it escaped Mrs. Slade. But she had grown bored with it by the time her husband made his big *coup* in Wall Street, and when they bought in upper Park Avenue had already begun to think: "I'd rather live opposite a speak-easy for a change; at least one might see it raided." The idea of seeing Grace raided was so amusing that (before the move) she launched it at a woman's lunch. It made a hit, and went the rounds—she sometimes wondered if it had crossed the street and reached Mrs. Ansley. She hoped not, but didn't much mind. Those were the days when respectability was at a discount, and it did the irreproachable no harm to laugh at them a little.

A few years later, and not many months apart, both ladies lost their husbands. There was an appropriate exchange of wreaths and condolences, and a brief renewal of intimacy in the half-shadow of their mourning; and now, after another interval, they had run across each other in Rome, at the same hotel, each of them the modest appendage of a salient daughter. The similarity of their lot had again drawn them together, lending itself to mild jokes, and the mutual confession that, if in old days it must have been tiring to "keep up" with daughters, it was now, at times, a little dull not to.

No doubt, Mrs. Slade reflected, she felt her unemployment more than poor Grace ever would. It was a big drop from being the wife of Delphin Slade to being his widow. She had always regarded herself (with a certain conjugal pride) as his equal in social gifts, as contributing her full share to the making of the exceptional couple they were: but the difference after his death was irremediable. As the wife of the famous corporation lawyer, always with an international case or two on hand, every day brought its exciting and unexpected obligation: the impromptu entertaining of eminent colleagues from abroad, the hurried dashes on legal business to London, Paris or Rome, where the entertaining was so handsomely reciprocated; the amusement of hearing in her wake: "What, that handsome woman with the good clothes and the eyes is Mrs. Slade—*the* Slade's wife? Really? Generally the wives of celebrities are such frumps."

Yes; being *the* Slade's widow was a dullish business after that. In living up to such a husband all her faculties had been engaged; now she had only her daughter to live up to, for the son who seemed to have inherited his father's gifts had died suddenly in boyhood. She had fought through that agony because her husband was there, to be helped and to help; now, after the father's death, the thought of the boy had become unbearable. There was nothing left but to mother her daughter; and dear Jenny was such a perfect daughter that she needed no excessive mothering. "Now with Babs Ansley I don't know that I *should* be so quiet," Mrs. Slade sometimes half-enviously reflected; but Jenny, who was younger than her brilliant friend, was that rare accident, an extremely pretty girl who somehow made youth and prettiness seem as safe as their absence. It was all perplexing—and to Mrs. Slade a little boring. She wished that Jenny would fall in love—with the wrong man, even; that she might have to be watched, out-manoeuvred, rescued. And instead, it was Jenny who watched her mother, kept her out of draughts, made sure that she had taken her tonic . . .

Mrs. Ansley was much less articulate than her friend, and her mental portrait of Mrs. Slade was slighter, and drawn with fainter touches. "Alida Slade's awfully brilliant; but not as brilliant as she thinks," would have summed it up; though she would have added, for the enlightenment of strangers, that Mrs. Slade had been an extremely dashing girl; much more so than her daughter, who was pretty, of course, and clever in a way, but had none of her mother's—well, "vividness," someone had once called it. Mrs. Ansley would take up current words like this and cite them in quotation marks, as unheard-of audacities. No; Jenny was not like her mother. Sometimes Mrs. Ansley thought Alida Slade was disappointed; on the whole she had had a sad life. Full of failures and mistakes; Mrs. Ansley had always been rather sorry for her. . . .

So these two ladies visualized each other, each through the wrong end of her little telescope.

II

For a long time they continued to sit side by side without speaking. It seemed as though, to both, there was a relief in laying down their somewhat futile activities in the presence of the vast Memento Mori which faced them. Mrs. Slade sat quite still, her eyes fixed on the golden slope of the Palace of the Caesars, and after a while Mrs. Ansley ceased to fidget with her bag, and she too sank into meditation. Like many intimate friends, the two ladies had never before had occasion to be silent together, and Mrs. Ansley was slightly embarrassed by what seemed, after so many years, a new stage in their intimacy, and one with which she did not yet know how to deal.

Suddenly the air was full of that deep clangour of bells which periodically covers Rome with a roof of silver. Mrs. Slade glanced at her wrist-watch. "Five o'clock already," she said, as though surprised.

Mrs. Ansley suggested interrogatively: "There's bridge at the Embassy at five." For a long time Mrs. Slade did not answer. She appeared to be lost in contemplation, and Mrs. Ansley thought the remark had escaped her. But after a while she said, as if speaking out of a dream: "Bridge, did you say? Not unless you want to . . . But I don't think I will, you know."

"Oh, no," Mrs. Ansley hastened to assure her. "I don't care to at all. It's so lovely here; and so full of old memories, as you say." She settled herself in her chair, and almost furtively drew forth her knitting. Mrs. Slade took sideways note of this activity, but her own beautifully cared for hands remained motionless on her knee.

"I was just thinking," she said slowly, "what different things Rome stands for to each generation of travellers. To our grandmothers, Roman fever; to our mothers, sentimental dangers—how we used to be guarded!; to our daughters, no more dangers than the middle of Main Street. They don't know it—but how much they're missing!"

The long golden light was beginning to pale, and Mrs. Ansley lifted her knitting a little closer to her eyes. "Yes; how we were guarded!"

"I always used to think," Mrs. Slade continued, "that our mothers had a much more difficult job than our grandmothers. When Roman fever stalked the streets it must have been comparatively easy to gather in the girls at the danger hour; but when you and I were young, with such beauty calling us, and the spice of disobedience thrown in, and no worse risk than catching cold during the cool hour after sunset, the mothers used to be put to it to keep us in—didn't they?"

She turned again toward Mrs. Ansley, but the latter had reached a delicate point in her knitting. "One, two, three— slip two; yes, they must have been," she assented, without looking up.

Mrs. Slade's eyes rested on her with a deepened attention. "She can knit—in the face of *this!* How like her . . ."

Mrs. Slade leaned back, brooding, her eyes ranging from the ruins which faced her to the long green hollow of the Forum, the fading glow of the church fronts beyond it, and the outlying immensity of the Colosseum. Suddenly she thought: "It's all very well to say that our girls have done away with sentiment and moonlight. But if Babs Ansley isn't out to catch that young aviator—the one who's a Marchese—then I don't know anything. And Jenny has no chance beside her. I know that too. I wonder if that's why Grace Ansley likes the two girls to go everywhere together? My poor Jenny as a foil—!" Mrs. Slade gave a hardly audible laugh, and at the sound Mrs. Ansley dropped her knitting.

"Yes—?"

"I—oh, nothing. I was only thinking how your Babs carries everything before her. That Campolieri boy is one of the best matches in Rome. Don't look so innocent, my dear—you know he is. And I was wondering, ever so respectfully, you understand . . . wondering how two such exemplary characters as you and Horace had managed to produce anything quite so dynamic." Mrs. Slade laughed again, with a touch of asperity.

Mrs. Ansley's hands lay inert across her needles. She looked straight out at the great accumulated wreckage of passion and splendour at her feet. But her small profile was almost expressionless. At length she said: "I think you overrate Babs, my dear."

Mrs. Slade's tone grew easier. "No; I don't. I appreciate her. And perhaps envy you. Oh, my girl's perfect; if I were a chronic invalid I'd—well, I think I'd rather be in Jenny's hands. There must be times . . . but there! I always wanted a brilliant daughter . . . and never quite understood why I got an angel instead."

Mrs. Ansley echoed her laugh in a faint murmur. "Babs is an angel too."

"Of course—of course! But she's got rainbow wings. Well, they're wandering by the sea with their young men; and here we sit . . . and it all brings back the past a little too acutely."

Mrs. Ansley had resumed her knitting. One might almost have imagined (if one had known her less well, Mrs. Slade reflected) that, for her also, too many memories rose from the lengthening shadows of those august ruins. But no; she was simply absorbed in her work. What was there for her to worry about? She knew that Babs would almost certainly come back engaged to the extremely eligible Campolieri. "And she'll sell the New York house, and settle down near them in Rome, and never be in their way . . . she's much too tactful.

But she'll have an excellent cook, and just the right people in for bridge and cocktails . . . and a perfectly peaceful old age among her grandchildren."

Mrs. Slade broke off this prophetic flight with a recoil of self-disgust. There was no one of whom she had less right to think unkindly than of Grace Ansley. Would she never cure herself of envying her? Perhaps she had begun too long ago.

She stood up and leaned against the parapet, filling her troubled eyes with the tranquillizing magic of the hour. But instead of tranquillizing her the sight seemed to increase her exasperation. Her gaze turned toward the Colosseum. Already its golden flank was drowned in purple shadow, and above it the sky curved crystal clear, without light or colour. It was the moment when afternoon and evening hang balanced in mid-heaven.

Mrs. Slade turned back and laid her hand on her friend's arm. The gesture was so abrupt that Mrs. Ansley looked up, startled.

"The sun's set. You're not afraid, my dear?"

"Afraid—"

"Of Roman fever or pneumonia? I remember how ill you were that winter. As a girl you had a very delicate throat, hadn't you?"

"Oh, we're all right up here. Down below, in the Forum, it does get deathly cold, all of a sudden . . . but not here."

"Ah, of course you know, because you had to be so careful." Mrs. Slade turned back to the parapet. She thought: "I must make one more effort not to hate her." Aloud she said: "Whenever I look at the Forum from up here, I remember that story about a great-aunt of yours, wasn't she? A dreadfully wicked great-aunt?"

"Oh, yes; Great-aunt Harriet. The one who was supposed to have sent her young sister out to the Forum after sunset to gather a night-blooming flower for her album. All our great-aunts and grand-mothers used to have albums of dried flowers."

Mrs. Slade nodded. "But she really sent her because they were in love with the same man—"

"Well, that was the family tradition. They said Aunt Harriet confessed it years afterward. At any rate, the poor little sister caught the fever and died. Mother used to frighten us with the story when we were children."

"And you frightened *me* with it, that winter when you and I were here as girls. The winter I was engaged to Delphin."

Mrs. Ansley gave a faint laugh. "Oh, did I? Really frightened you? I don't believe you're easily frightened."

"Not often; but I was then. I was easily frightened because I was too happy. I wonder if you know what that means?"

"I—yes . . . ," Mrs. Ansley faltered.

"Well, I suppose that was why the story of your wicked aunt made such an impression on me. And I thought: 'There's no more Roman fever, but the Forum is deathly cold after sunset—especially after a hot day. And the Colosseum's even colder and damper.' "

"The Colosseum—?"

"Yes. It wasn't easy to get in, after the gates were locked for the night. Far from easy. Still, in those days it could be managed; it *was* managed, often. Lovers met there who couldn't meet elsewhere. You knew that?"

"I—I daresay. I don't remember."

"You don't remember? You don't remember going to visit some ruins or other one evening, just after dark, and catching a bad chill? You were supposed to have gone to see the moon rise. People always said that expedition was what caused your illness."

There was a moment's silence; then Mrs. Ansley rejoined: "Did they? It was all so long ago."

"Yes. And you got well again—so it didn't matter. But I suppose it struck your friends—the reason given for your illness, I mean—because everybody knew you were so prudent on account of your throat, and your mother took such care of you . . . You *had* been out late sight-seeing, hadn't you, that night?"

"Perhaps I had. The most prudent girls aren't always prudent. What made you think of it now?"

Mrs. Slade seemed to have no answer ready. But after a moment she broke out: "Because I simply can't bear it any longer—!"

Mrs. Ansley lifted her head quickly. Her eyes were wide and very pale. "Can't bear what?"

"Why—your not knowing that I've always known why you went."

"Why I went—?"

"Yes. You think I'm bluffing, don't you? Well, you went to meet the man I was engaged to—and I can repeat every word of the letter that took you there."

While Mrs. Slade spoke, Mrs. Ansley had risen unsteadily to her feet. Her bag, her knitting and gloves slid in a panic-stricken heap to the ground. She looked at Mrs. Slade as though she were looking at a ghost.

"No, no—don't," she faltered out.

"Why not? Listen, if you don't believe me. 'My one darling, things can't go on like this. I must see you alone. Come to the Colosseum immediately after dark tomorrow. There will be somebody to let you in. No one whom you need fear will suspect'—but perhaps you've forgotten what the letter said?"

Mrs. Ansley met the challenge with an unexpected composure. Steadying herself against the chair, she looked at her friend and replied: "No; I know it by heart too."

"And the signature? 'Only *your* D.S.' Was that it? I'm

right, am I not? That was the letter that took you out that evening after dark?"

Mrs. Ansley was still looking at her. It seemed to Mrs. Slade that a slow struggle was going on behind the voluntarily controlled mask of her small quiet face. "I shouldn't have thought she had herself so well in hand," Mrs. Slade reflected, almost resentfully. But at this moment Mrs. Ansley spoke. "I don't know how you knew. I burnt that letter at once."

"Yes; you would, naturally—you're so prudent!" The sneer was open now. "And if you burnt the letter, you're wondering how on earth I know what was in it. That's it, isn't it?"

Mrs. Slade waited, but Mrs. Ansley did not speak.

"Well, my dear, I know what was in that letter because I wrote it!"

"You wrote it?"

"Yes."

The two women stood for a minute staring at each other in the last golden light. Then Mrs. Ansley dropped back into her chair. "Oh," she murmured, and covered her face with her hands.

Mrs. Slade waited nervously for another word or movement. None came, and at length she broke out: "I horrify you."

Mrs. Ansley's hands dropped to her knee. The face they uncovered was streaked with tears. "I wasn't thinking of you. I was thinking—it was the only letter I ever had from him!"

"And I wrote it. Yes; I wrote it! But I was the girl he was engaged to. Did you happen to remember that?"

Mrs. Ansley's head drooped again. "I'm not trying to excuse myself . . . I remembered . . ."

"And still you went?"

"Still I went."

Mrs. Slade stood looking down on the small bowed figure at her side. The flame of her wrath had already sunk, and she wondered why she had ever thought there would be any satisfaction in inflicting so purposeless a wound on her friend. But she had to justify herself.

"You do understand? I'd found out—and I hated you, hated you. I knew you were in love with Delphin—and I was afraid; afraid of you, of your quiet ways, your sweetness . . . your . . . well, I wanted you out of the way, that's all. Just for a few weeks; just till I was sure of him. So in a blind fury I wrote that letter. . . . I don't know why I'm telling you now."

"I suppose," said Mrs. Ansley slowly, "it's because you've always gone on hating me."

"Perhaps. Or because I wanted to get the whole thing off my mind." She paused. "I'm glad you destroyed the letter. Of course I never thought you'd die."

Mrs. Ansley relapsed into silence, and Mrs. Slade, leaning above her, was conscious of a strange sense of isolation, of being cut off from the warm current of human communion. "You think me a monster!"

"I don't know. . . . It was the only letter I had, and you say he didn't write it?"

"Ah, how you care for him still!"

"I cared for that memory," said Mrs. Ansley.

Mrs. Slade continued to look down on her. She seemed physically reduced by the blow—as if, when she got up, the wind might scatter her like a puff of dust. Mrs. Slade's jealousy suddenly leapt up again at the sight. All these years the woman had been living on that letter. How she must have loved him, to treasure the mere memory of its ashes! The letter of the man her friend was engaged to. Wasn't it she who was the monster?

"You tried your best to get him away from me, didn't you? But you failed; and I kept him. That's all."

"Yes. That's all."

"I wish now I hadn't told you. I'd no idea you'd feel about it as you do; I thought you'd be amused. It all happened so long ago, as you say; and you must do me the justice to remember that I had no reason to think you'd ever taken it seriously. How could I, when you were married to Horace Ansley two months afterward? As soon as you could get out of bed your mother rushed you off to Florence and married you. People were rather surprised—they wondered at its being done so quickly; but I thought I knew. I had an idea you did it out of *pique*—to be able to say you'd got ahead of Delphin and me. Girls have such silly reasons for doing the most serious things. And your marrying so soon convinced me that you'd never really cared."

"Yes. I suppose it would," Mrs. Ansley assented.

The clear heaven overhead was emptied of all its gold. Dusk spread over it, abruptly darkening the Seven Hills. Here and there lights began to twinkle through the foliage at their feet. Steps were coming and going on the deserted terrace—waiters looking out of the doorway at the head of the stairs, then reappearing with trays and napkins and flasks of wine. Tables were moved, chairs straightened. A feeble string of electric lights flickered out. Some vases of faded flowers were carried away, and brought back replenished. A stout lady in a dust-coat suddenly appeared, asking in broken Italian if anyone had seen the elastic band which held together her tattered Baedeker. She poked with her stick under the table at which she had lunched, the waiters assisting.

The corner where Mrs. Slade and Mrs. Ansley sat was still shadowy and deserted. For a long time neither of them spoke. At length Mrs. Slade began again: "I suppose I did it as a sort of joke—"

"A joke?"

"Well, girls are ferocious sometimes, you know. Girls in love especially. And I remember laughing to myself all that evening at the idea that you were waiting around there in the dark, dodging out of sight, listening for every sound, trying to get in—Of course I was upset when I heard you were so ill afterward."

Mrs. Ansley had not moved for a long time. But now she turned slowly toward her companion. "But I didn't wait. He'd arranged everything. He was there. We were let in at once," she said.

Mrs. Slade sprang up from her leaning position. "Delphin there? They let you in?—Ah, now you're lying!" she burst out with violence.

Mrs. Ansley's voice grew clearer, and full of surprise. "But of course he was there. Naturally he came—"

"Came? How did he know he'd find you there? You must be raving!"

Mrs. Ansley hesitated, as though reflecting. "But I answered the letter. I told him I'd be there. So he came."

Mrs. Slade flung her hands up to her face. "Oh, God—you answered! I never thought of your answering . . ."

"It's odd you never thought of it, if you wrote the letter."

"Yes. I was blind with rage."

Mrs. Ansley rose, and drew her fur scarf about her. "It is cold here. We'd better go . . . I'm sorry for you," she said, as she clasped the fur about her throat.

The unexpected words sent a pang through Mrs. Slade. "Yes; we'd better go." She gathered up her bag and cloak. "I don't know why you should be sorry for me," she muttered.

Mrs. Ansley stood looking away from her toward the dusky secret mass of the Colosseum. "Well—because I didn't have to wait that night."

Mrs. Slade gave an unquiet laugh. "Yes; I was beaten there. But I oughtn't to begrudge it to you, I suppose. At the end of all these years. After all, I had everything; I had him for twenty-five years. And you had nothing but that one letter that he didn't write."

Mrs. Ansley was again silent. At length she turned toward the door of the terrace. She took a step and turned back, facing her companion.

"I had Barbara," she said, and began to move ahead of Mrs. Slade toward the stairway.

And Don't Forget the One Red Rose

by Avram Davidson

Charley Barton was the staff of an East New York establishment that supplied used gas stoves on a wholesale basis. He received deliveries at the back door, dollied them inside, took them apart, cleaned them (and cleaned them and cleaned them and cleaned them) till they sparkled as much as their generally rundown nature would allow, fitted on missing parts and set them up in front of the place, where they might be chaffered over by prospective buyers.

He never handled sales. These were taken care of by his employer, a thickset and neckless individual who was there only part of the time. When not fawning upon the proprietors of retail used-appliance stores, he was being brutal to Charley. This man's name was Matt Mungo, and he arrived in neat, middle-class clothes from what he referred to as his "other place," never further described to Charley, who did not venture to be curious.

Charley doubted, however, that Mungo did—indeed, he was certain that Mungo did not—display to employees and patrons of his other place the insulting manner and methods he used in the stove warehouse.

Besides calling Charley many offensive names in many offensive ways, Mungo had the habit of shoving him, poking him and generally pushing him around. Did Charley, goaded beyond patience, pause or turn to complain, Mungo, pretending great surprise, would demand, "What? *What?*"— and, before Charley could formulate his protest, he would swiftly thrust stiff thick fingers into Charley's side or stomach and dart away to a distance, whence he would loudly and abusively call attention to work he desired done, and which Charley would certainly have done anyway in the natural course of things.

Charley lived on the second floor of an old and unpicturesque building a few blocks from the warehouse. On the first floor lived two old women who dressed in black, who had no English and went often to church. On the top floor lived an Asian man about whom Charley knew nothing. That is, he knew nothing until one evening when, returning from work and full of muscular aches and pains and resentments, he saw this man trying to fit a card into the frame of the name plate over the man's doorbell in the downstairs entrance. The frame was bent; the card resisted; Charley pulled out a rather long knife and jimmied the ancient and warped piece of metal; the card slipped in. And the Asian man said, "Thank you, so."

"Oh, that's all right," and Charley looked to see what the name might be. But the card said only BOOK STORE. "Funny place for a store," Charley said. "But maybe you expect to do most of your business by mail, I guess."

"No, oh," the Asian man said. And, with a slight bow, a slight smile and a slight gesture, he urged Charley to precede him up the stairs in the dark and smelly hall. About

94

halfway up the first flight, the Asian man said, "I extend you to enjoy a cup of tea and a tobacco cigarette whilst in my so newly opened sales place."

"Why, sure," said Charley instantly. "Why, thank you very much." Social invitations came seldom to him and, to tell the truth, he was rather ugly, slow and stupid—facts that were often pointed out by Mungo. He now asked, "Are you Chinese or Japanese?"

"No," said his neighbor. And he said nothing else until they were on the top floor, when, after unlocking the door and slipping in his hand to flip on the light switch, he gestured to his downstairs co-resident to enter, with the word "Do."

It was certainly unlike any of the bookstores to which Charley was accustomed . . . in that he was accustomed to them at all. Instead of open shelves, there were cabinets against the walls, and there were a number of wooden chests as well. Mr. Book Store did not blow upon embers to make the tea; he poured it, already sweetened, from a Thermos bottle into a plastic cup, and the cigarette was a regular American cigarette. When tea and tobacco had been consumed, he began to open the chests and the cabinets. First he took out a very, very tiny book in a very, very strange-looking language. "I never saw paper like that before," Charley said.

"It is factually palm leaf. A Buddhist litany. Soot is employed, instead of ink, in marking the text. Is it not precious?"

Charley nodded and politely asked, "How much does it cost?"

The bookman examined an odd-looking tag. "The price of it," he said, "is a bar of silver the weight of a newborn child." He removed it gently from Charley's hand, replaced

95

it in the pigeonhole in the cabinet, closed the cabinet, lifted the carven lid of an aromatic chest and took out something larger, much larger, and wrapped in cloth of tissue of gold. "Edition of great illustrated work on the breeding of elephants in captivity, on yellow paper smoored with alum in wavy pattern; most rare; agreed?"

For one thing, Charley hardly felt in a position to disagree; and, for another, he was greatly surprised and titillated by the next illustration. "Hey, look at what that one is *do*ing!" he exclaimed.

The bookman looked. A faint, indulgent smile creased his ivory face. "Droll," he commented. He moved to take it back.

"How much does *this* one cost?"

The dealer scrutinized the tag. "The price of this one," he said, "is set down as 'A pair of white parrots, an embroidered robe of purple, sixty-seven fine inlaid vessels of beaten gold, one hundred platters of silver filigree work and ten catties of cardamoms.' " He removed the book, rewrapped it and restored it to its place in the chest.

"Did you bring them all from your own country, then?"

"All," said the Asian man, nodding. "Treasures of my ancestors, broughten across the ice-fraught Himalayan passes upon the backs of yaks. Perilous journey." He gestured. "All which remains, tangibly, of ancient familial culture."

Charley made a sympathetic squint and said, "Say, that's too bad. Say! *I* remember now! In the newspapers! Tibetan refugees—you must have fled from the approaching Chinese Communists!"

The bookman shook his head. "Factually, not. Non-Tibetan. Flight was from approaching forces of rapacious Dhu thA Hmy'egh, wicked and dissident vassal of the king of Bhutan. As way to Bhutan proper was not available,

96

escape was into India." He considered, withdrew another item from another chest.

"Well, you speak very good English."

"Instructed in tutorial fashion by late the Oliver Blunt-Piggot, disgarbed shaman of a Christian fane in Poona." He lifted the heavy board cover of a very heavy volume.

"When was this?"

"Ago." He set down the cover, slowly turned the huge, thick pages. "Perceive, barbarians in native costume, bringing tribute." Charley had definite ideas as to what was polite, expected. He might not be able to, could hardly expect to buy. But it was only decent to act as though he could. Only thus could he show interest. And so, again, ask he did.

Again, the bookman's pale slim fingers sought the tag. "Ah, mm. The price of this is one mummified simurgh enwrapped in six bolts of pale brocade, an hundred measures of finest musk in boxes of granulated goldwork and a viper of Persia pickled in Venetian treacle." He replaced the pages, set back the cover and set to rewrapping.

Charley, after some thought, asked if all the books had prices like that. "Akk, yes. All these books have such prices, which are the exceedingly carefully calculated evaluations established by my ancestors in the High Vale of Lhom-bhya—formerly the Crossroads of the World, before the earthquake buried most of the passes, thus diverting trade to Lhasa, Samarkand and such places. So."

A question that had gradually been taking form in the shape of a wrinkle now found verbal expression. "But couldn't you just sell them for *money?*"

The bookman touched the tip of his nose with the tip of his middle finger. "For money? Let me have thought. . . . Ah! Here is *The Book of Macaws, Egrets and Francolins*, in the Five Colors, for only eighty-three gold mohurs from the mint of Baber Mogul and one silver dirhem of Aaron the Righteous. . . . You call him Aaron the Righteous? Not. Pardon. Harun al-Rashid. A bargain."

Charley shook his head. "No, I mean, just ordinary money."

The bookdealer bowed and shook his own head. "Neighboring sir," he said, "I have not twenty-seven times risked my life, nor suffered pangs and pains innumerable, merely to sell for ordinary money these treasures handed down from my progenitors, nor ignore their noble standards of value. Oh, nay." And he restored to its container *The Book of Macaws, Egrets and Francolins.* In the Five Colors.

A certain stubbornness crept over Charley. "Well, then, what is the cheapest one you've got, then?" he demanded.

The scion of the High Vale of Lhom-bhya shrugged, fingered his lower lip, looked here and there, uttered a slight and soft exclamation and took from the last cabinet in the far corner an immense scroll. It had rollers of chalcedony with ivory finials and a case of scented *samal-*wood lacquered in vermilion and picked with gold; its cord weights were of banded agate.

"This is a mere diversion for the idle moments of a prince. In abridged form, its title reads, *Book of Precious Secrets on How to Make Silver and Gold from Dust, Dung and Bran; Also How to Obtain the Affections; Plus One Hundred and Thirty-Eight Attitudes for Carnal Conjunction and Sixty Recipes for Substances Guaranteed to Maintain the Stance as Well as Tasting Good: by a Sage.*" He opened the scroll and slowly began to unwind it over the length of the table.

The pictures were of the most exquisitely detailed workmanship and brilliant of color on which crushed gold quartz had been sprinkled while the glorious pigments were as yet still wet. Charley's heart gave a great bound, then sank. "No, I said the *cheapest* one———"

His host stifled a very slight yawn. "This is the cheapest," he said, indifferent, almost. "What is cheaper than lust or of less value than alchemy or aphrodisiacs? The price . . . the price," he said, examining the tag, which was of ebony inlaid with jasper. "The price is the crushed head of a sandal merchant of Babylon, with a red, red rose between his teeth: a trifle. The precise utility of that escapes me, but it is of no matter. My only task is to obtain the price as established— that and, of course, to act as your host until the stars turn pale."

Charley rose. "I guess I'll be going, anyway," he said. "I certainly want to thank you for showing me all this. Maybe I'll be back tomorrow for something, if they haven't all been sold by then." His heart knew what his heart desired, his head knew the impossibility of any of it, but his lips at least maintained a proper politeness even at the last.

He went down the stairs, his mind filled with odd thoughts, half enjoyable, half despairing. Heavy footsteps sounded coming up; who was it but Mungo. "I thought you said you lived on the *second* floor," he said. "No use lying to *me;* come on, dumbbell, I need you. Earn your goddamn money for a change. My funking car's got a flat; *move* it, I tell you, spithead; when I say move it, you *move* it!" And he jabbed his thick, stiff fingers into Charley's kidneys and, ignoring his employee's cry of pain, half guided, half goaded him along the empty blocks to the empty block lined with closed warehouses where, indeed, an automobile stood, somewhat sagging to one side.

"Get the goddamn jack up; what're you dreaming about? Quite stumbling over your goddamn feet, for cry-sake; you think I got nothing better to do? You think I do nothing but sell greasy stoves to greaseballs? *Move* it, nipplehead! I want you to know that I also own the biggest goddamn shoe store in Babylon, Long Island. Pick up that tire iron!"

The Men Who Murdered Mohammed
by Alfred Bester

There was a man who mutilated history. He toppled empires and uprooted dynasties. Because of him, Mount Vernon should not be a national shrine, and Columbus, Ohio, should be called Cabot, Ohio. Because of him the name Marie Curie should be cursed in France, and no one should swear by the beard of the Prophet. Actually, these realities did not happen, because he was a mad professor; or, to put it another way, he only succeeded in making them unreal for himself.

Now, the patient reader is too familiar with the conventional mad professor, undersized and overbrowed, creating monsters in his laboratory which invariably turn on their maker and menace his lovely daughter. This story isn't about that sort of make-believe man. It's about Henry Hassel, a genuine mad professor in a class with such better-known men as Ludwig Boltzmann (*see* Ideal Gas Law), Jacques Charles and André Marie Ampère (1775–1836).

Everyone ought to know that the electrical ampere was so

named in honor of Ampère. Ludwig Boltzmann was a distinguished Austrian physicist, as famous for his research on black-body radiation as on Ideal Gases. You can look him up in Volume Three of the *Encyclopaedia Britannica*, BALT to BRAI. Jacques Alexandre César Charles was the first mathematician to become interested in flight, and he invented the hydrogen balloon. These were real men.

They were also real mad professors. Ampère, for example, was on his way to an important meeting of scientists in Paris. In his taxi he got a brilliant idea (of an electrical nature, I assume) and whipped out a pencil and jotted the equation on the wall of the hansom cab. Roughly, it was: $dH = ipdl/r^2$ in which p is the perpendicular distance from P to the line of the element dl; or $dH = i\,sin\phi\,dl/r^2$. This is sometimes known as Laplace's Law, although he wasn't at the meeting.

Anyway, the cab arrived at the Académie. Ampère jumped out, paid the driver and rushed into the meeting to tell everybody about his idea. Then he realized he didn't have the note on him, remembered where he'd left it, and had to chase through the streets of Paris after the taxi to recover his runaway equation. Sometimes I imagine that's how Fermat lost his famous "Last Theorem," although Fermat wasn't at the meeting either, having died some two hundred years earlier.

Or take Boltzmann. Giving a course in Advanced Ideal Gases, he peppered his lectures with involved calculus, which he worked out quickly and casually in his head. He had that kind of head. His students had so much trouble trying to puzzle out the math by ear that they couldn't keep up with the lectures, and they begged Boltzmann to work out his equations on the blackboard.

Boltzmann apologized and promised to be more helpful in the future. At the next lecture he began, "Gentlemen, com-

101

bining Boyle's Law with the Law of Charles, we arrive at the equation $pv = p_0v_0 (1 + at)$. Now, obviously, if $_aS^b = f(x) \, dx \, (a)$, then $pv = RT$ and $Sf(x,y,z) \, dV = 0$. It's as simple as two plus two equals four." At this point Boltzmann remembered his promise. He turned to the blackboard, conscientiously chalked $2 + 2 = 4$, and then breezed on, casually doing the complicated calculus in his head.

Jacques Charles, the brilliant mathematician who discovered Charles' Law (sometimes known as Gay-Lussac's Law), which Boltzmann mentioned in his lecture, had a lunatic passion to become a famous paleographer—that is, a discoverer of ancient manuscripts. I think that being forced to share credit with Gay-Lussac may have unhinged him.

He paid a transparent swindler named Vrain-Lucas 200,000 francs for holograph letters purportedly written by Julius Caesar, Alexander the Great, and Pontius Pilate. Charles, a man who could see through any gas, ideal or not, actually believed in these forgeries despite the fact that the maladroit Vrain-Lucas had written them in modern French on modern notepaper bearing modern watermarks. Charles even tried to donate them to the Louvre.

Now, these men weren't idiots. They were geniuses who paid a high price for their genius because the rest of their thinking was other-world. A genius is someone who travels to truth by an unexpected path. Unfortunately, unexpected paths lead to disaster in everyday life. This is what happened to Henry Hassel, professor of Applied Compulsion at Unknown University in the year 1980.

Nobody knows where Unknown University is or what they teach there. It has a faculty of some two hundred eccentrics, and a student body of two thousand misfits—the kind that remain anonymous until they win Nobel prizes or become the First Man on Mars. You can always spot a graduate of

U.U. when you ask people where they went to school. If you get an evasive reply like: "State," or "Oh, a fresh-water school you never heard of," you can bet they went to Unknown. Someday I hope to tell you more about this university, which is a center of learning only in the Pickwickian sense.

Anyway, Henry Hassel started home from his office in the Psychotic Psenter early one afternoon, strolling through the Physical Culture arcade. It is not true that he did this to leer at the nude coeds practicing Arcane Eurythmics; rather, Hassel liked to admire the trophies displayed in the arcade in memory of great Unknown teams which had won the sort of championships that Unknown teams win—in sports like Strabismus, Occlusion and Botulism. (Hassel had been Frambesia singles champion three years running.) He arrived home uplifted, and burst gaily into the house to discover his wife in the arms of a man.

There she was, a lovely woman of thirty-five, with smoky red hair and almond eyes, being heartily embraced by a person whose pockets were stuffed with pamphlets, microchemical apparatus and a patella-reflex hammer—a typical campus character of U.U., in fact. The embrace was so concentrated that neither of the offending parties noticed Henry Hassel glaring at them from the hallway.

Now, remember Ampère and Charles and Boltzmann. Hassel weighed one hundred and ninety pounds. He was muscular and uninhibited. It would have been child's play for him to have dismembered his wife and her lover, and thus simply and directly to have achieved the goal he desired— the end of his wife's life. But Henry Hassel was in the genius class; his mind just didn't operate that way.

Hassel breathed hard, turned and lumbered into his private laboratory like a freight engine. He opened a drawer labeled DUODENUM and removed a .45-caliber revolver. He opened other drawers, more interestingly labeled, and assembled apparatus. In exactly seven and one-half minutes (such was his rage) he put together a time machine (such was his genius).

Professor Hassel assembled the time machine around him, set a dial for 1902, picked up the revolver and pressed a button. The machine made a noise like defective plumbing, and Hassel disappeared. He reappeared in Philadelphia on June 3, 1902, went directly to No. 1218 Walnut Street, a red-brick house with marble steps, and rang the bell. A man who might have passed for the third Smith Brother opened the door and looked at Henry Hassel.

"Mr. Jessup?" Hassel asked in a suffocated voice.

"Yes?"

"You are Mr. Jessup?"

"I am."

"You will have a son, Edgar? Edgar Allan Jessup—so named because of your regrettable admiration for Poe?"

The third Smith Brother was startled. "Not that I know of," he said. "I'm not married yet."

"You will be," Hassel said angrily. "I have the misfortune to be married to your son's daughter, Greta. Excuse me." He raised the revolver and shot his wife's grandfather-to-be.

"She will have ceased to exist," Hassel muttered, blowing smoke out of the revolver. "I'll be a bachelor. I may even be married to somebody else. . . . Good God! Who?"

Hassel waited impatiently for the automatic recall of the time machine to snatch him back to his own laboratory. He rushed into his living room. There was his redheaded wife, still in the arms of a man.

Hassel was thunderstruck.

"So that's it," he growled. "A family tradition of faithlessness. Well, we'll see about that. We have ways and means." He permitted himself a hollow laugh, returned to his laboratory, and sent himself back to the year 1901, where he shot and killed Emma Hotchkiss, his wife's maternal grand-mother-to-be. He returned to his own home in his own time. There was his redheaded wife, still in the arms of another man.

"But I *know* the old bitch was her grandmother," Hassel muttered. "You couldn't miss the resemblance. What the hell's gone wrong?"

Hassel was confused and dismayed, but not without resources. He went to his study, had difficulty picking up the phone, but finally managed to dial the Malpractice Laboratory. His finger kept oozing out of the dial holes.

"Sam?" he said. "This is Henry."

"Who?"

"Henry."

"You'll have to speak up."

"Henry Hassel!"

"Oh, good afternoon, Henry."

"Tell me all about time."

"Time? Hmmm . . ." The Simplex-and-Multiplex Computer cleared its throat while it waited for the data circuits to link up. "Ahem. Time. (1) Absolute. (2) Relative. (3) Recurrent. (1) Absolute: period, contingent, duration, diurnity, perpetuity—"

"Sorry, Sam. Wrong request. Go back. I want time, reference to succession of, travel in."

Sam shifted gears and began again. Hassel listened intently. He nodded. He grunted. "Uh huh. Uh huh. Right. I see. Thought so. A continuum, eh? Acts performed in past must alter future. Then I'm on the right track. But act must be significant, eh? Mass-action effect. Trivia cannot divert existing phenomena streams. Hmmm. But how trivial is a grandmother?"

"What are you trying to do, Henry?"

"Kill my wife," Hassel snapped. He hung up. He returned to his laboratory. He considered, still in a jealous rage.

"Got to do something significant," he muttered. "Wipe Greta out. Wipe it all out. All right, by God! I'll show 'em."

Hassel went back to the year 1775, visited a Virginia farm and shot a young colonel in the brisket. The colonel's name was George Washington, and Hassel made sure he was dead. He returned to his own time and his own home. There was his redheaded wife, still in the arms of another.

"Damn!" said Hassel. He was running out of ammunition. He opened a fresh box of cartridges, went back in time and massacred Christopher Columbus, Napoleon, Mohammed and half a dozen other celebrities. "That ought to do it, by God!" said Hassel.

He returned to his own time, and found his wife as before.

His knees turned to water; his feet seemed to melt into the floor. He went back to his laboratory, walking through nightmare quicksands.

"What the hell is significant?" Hassel asked himself painfully. "How much does it take to change futurity? By God, I'll really change it this time. I'll go for broke."

He traveled to Paris at the turn of the twentieth century and visited a Madame Curie in an attic workshop near the Sorbonne. "Madame," he said in his execrable French, "I am a stranger to you of the utmost, but a scientist entire. Knowing of your experiments with radium— Oh? You haven't got to radium yet? No matter. I am here to teach you all of nuclear fission."

He taught her. He had the satisfaction of seeing Paris go up in a mushroom of smoke before the automatic recall brought him home. "That'll teach women to be faithless," he growled. . . . "Guhhh!" The last was wrenched from his lips when he saw his redheaded wife still— But no need to belabor the obvious.

Hassel swam through fogs to his study and sat down to think. While he's thinking I'd better warn you that this is not a conventional time story. If you imagine for a moment that Henry is going to discover that the man fondling his wife is himself, you're mistaken. The viper is not Henry Hassel, his son, a relation, or even Ludwig Boltzmann (1844–1906). Hassel does not make a circle in time, ending where the story begins—to the satisfaction of nobody and the fury of everybody—for the simple reason that time isn't circular, or linear, or tandem, discoid, syzygous, longinquitous, or pandiculated. Time is a private matter, as Hassel discovered.

"Maybe I slipped up somehow," Hassel muttered. "I'd better find out." He fought with the telephone, which seemed to weigh a hundred tons, and at last managed to get through to the library.

"Hello, Library? This is Henry."

"Who?"

"Henry Hassel."

"Speak up, please."

"HENRY HASSEL!"

"Oh. Good afternoon, Henry."

"What have you got on George Washington?"

Library clucked while her scanners sorted through her catalogues. "George Washington, first president of the United States, was born in—"

"First president? Wasn't he murdered in 1775?"

"Really, Henry. That's an absurd question. Everybody knows that George Wash—"

"Doesn't anybody know he was shot?"

"By whom?"

"Me."

"When?"

"In 1775."

"How did you manage to do that?"

"I've got a revolver."

"No, I mean, how did you do it two hundred years ago?"

"I've got a time machine."

"Well, there's no record here," Library said. "He's still doing fine in my files. You must have missed."

"I did not miss. What about Christopher Columbus? Any record of his death in 1489?"

"But he discovered the New World in 1492."

"He did not. He was murdered in 1489."

"How?"

"With a forty-five slug in the gizzard."

"You again, Henry?"

"Yes."

"There's no record here," Library insisted. "You must be one lousy shot."

"I will not lose my temper," Hassel said in a trembling voice.

"Why not, Henry?"

"Because it's lost already!" he shouted. "All right! What about Marie Curie? Did she or did she not discover the fission bomb which destroyed Paris at the turn of the century?"

"She did not. Enrico Fermi—"

"She did."

"She didn't."

"I personally taught her. Me. Henry Hassel."

"Everybody says you're a wonderful theoretician, but a lousy teacher, Henry. You—"

"Go to hell, you old biddy. This has got to be explained."

"Why?"

"I forget. There was something on my mind, but it doesn't matter now. What would you suggest?"

"You really have a time machine?"

"Of course I've got a time machine."

"Then go back and check."

Hassel returned to the year 1775, visited Mount Vernon, and interrupted the spring planting. "Excuse me, Colonel," he began.

The big man looked at him curiously. "You talk funny, stranger," he said. "Where are you from?"

"Oh, a fresh-water school you never heard of."

"You look funny too. Kind of misty, so to speak."

"Tell me, Colonel, what do you hear from Christopher Columbus?"

"Not much," Colonel Washington answered. "Been dead two, three hundred years."

"When did he die?"

"Year fifteen hundred some-odd, near as I remember."

"He did not. He died in 1489."

"Got your dates wrong, friend. He discovered America in 1492."

"Cabot discovered America. Sebastian Cabot."

"Nope. Cabot came a mite later."

"I have infallible proof!" Hassel began, but broke off as a stocky and rather stout man with a face ludicrously reddened by rage approached. He was wearing baggy gray slacks and a tweed jacket two sizes too small for him. He was carrying a .45 revolver. It was only after he had stared for a moment that Henry Hassel realized that he was looking at himself and not relishing the sight.

"My God!" Hassel murmured. "It's me, coming back to murder Washington that first time. If I'd made this second trip an hour later, I'd have found Washington dead. Hey!" he called. "Not yet. Hold off a minute. I've got to straighten something out first."

Hassel paid no attention to himself; indeed, he did not appear to be aware of himself. He marched straight up to Colonel Washington and shot him in the gizzard. Colonel Washington collapsed, emphatically dead. The first murderer inspected the body and then, ignoring Hassel's attempt to stop him and engage him in dispute, turned and marched off, muttering venomously to himself.

"He didn't hear me," Hassel wondered. "He didn't even feel me. And why don't I remember myself trying to stop me the first time I shot the colonel? What the hell is going on?"

Considerably disturbed, Henry Hassel visited Chicago and dropped into the Chicago University squash courts in the early 1940s. There, in a slippery mess of graphite bricks and graphite dust that coated him, he located an Italian scientist named Fermi.

"Repeating Marie Curie's work, I see, *dottore?*" Hassel said.

Fermi glanced about as though he had heard a faint sound.

"Repeating Marie Curie's work, *dottore?*" Hassel roared.

Fermi looked at him strangely. "Where you from, *amico?*"

"State."

"State Department?"

"Just State. It's true, isn't it, *dottore*, that Marie Curie discovered nuclear fission back in nineteen ought ought?"

"No! No! No!" Fermi cried. "We are the first, and we are not there yet. Police! Police! Spy!"

"This time I'll go on record," Hassel growled. He pulled out his trusty .45, emptied it into Dr. Fermi's chest, and awaited arrest and immolation in newspaper files. To his amazement, Dr. Fermi did not collapse. Dr. Fermi merely explored his chest tenderly and, to the men who answered his cry, said, "It is nothing. I felt in my within a sudden sensation of burn which may be a neuralgia of the cardiac nerve, but is most likely gas."

Hassel was too agitated to wait for the automatic recall of the time machine. Instead he returned at once to Unknown University under his own power. This should have given him a clue, but he was too possessed to notice. It was at this time that I (1913–1975) first saw him—a dim figure tramping through parked cars, closed doors and brick walls, with the light of lunatic determination on his face.

He oozed into the library, prepared for an exhaustive discussion, but could not make himself felt or heard by the catalogues. He went to the Malpractice Laboratory, where Sam, the Simplex-and-Multiplex Computer, has installations sensitive up to 10,700 angstroms. Sam could not see Henry, but managed to hear him through a sort of wave-interference phenomenon.

"Sam," Hassel said, "I've made one hell of a discovery."

"You're always making discoveries, Henry," Sam complained. "Your data allocation is filled. Do I have to start another tape for you?"

"But I need advice. Who's the leading authority on time, reference to succession of, travel in?"

"That would be Israel Lennox, spatial mechanics, professor of, Yale."

"How do I get in touch with him?"

"You don't, Henry. He's dead. Died in '75."

"What authority have you got on time, travel in, living?"

"Wiley Murphy."

"Murphy? From your own Trauma Department? That's a break. Where is he now?"

"As a matter of fact, Henry, he went over to your house to ask you something."

Hassel went home without walking, searched through his laboratory and study without finding anyone, and at last floated into the living room, where his redheaded wife was still in the arms of another man. (All this, you understand, had taken place within the space of a few moments after the construction of the time machine; such is the nature of time and time travel.) Hassel cleared his throat once or twice and tried to tap his wife on the shoulder. His fingers went through her.

"Excuse me, darling," he said. "Has Wiley Murphy been in to see me?"

Then he looked closer and saw that the man embracing his wife was Murphy himself.

"Murphy!" Hassel exclaimed. "The very man I'm looking for. I've had the most extraordinary experience." Hassel at once launched into a lucid description of his extraordinary experience, which went something like this: "Murphy, $u - v = (u^{\frac{1}{2}} - v^{\frac{1}{4}}) (u^a + u^x v^y + v^b)$ but when George Washington $F(x)y^2\,dx$ and Enrico Fermi $F(u^{\frac{1}{2}})\,dxdt$ one half of Marie Curie, then what about Christopher Columbus times the square root of minus one?"

Murphy ignored Hassel, as did Mrs. Hassel. I jotted down Hassel's equations on the hood of a passing taxi.

"Do listen to me, Murphy," Hassel said. "Greta dear, would you mind leaving us for a moment? I— For heaven's sake, will you two stop that nonsense? This is serious."

Hassel tried to separate the couple. He could no more touch them than make them hear him. His face turned red again and he became quite choleric as he beat at Mrs. Hassel and Murphy. It was like beating an Ideal Gas. I thought it best to interfere.

"Hassel!"

"Who's that?"

"Come outside a moment. I want to talk to you."

He shot through the wall. "Where are you?"

"Over here."

"You're sort of dim."

"So are you."

"Who are you?"

"My name's Lennox. Israel Lennox."

"Israel Lennox, spatial mechanics, professor of, Yale?"

"The same."

"But you died in '75."

112

"I disappeared in '75."

"What d'you mean?"

"I invented a time machine."

"By God! So did I," Hassel said. "This afternoon. The idea came to me in a flash—I don't know why—and I've had the most extraordinary experience. Lennox, time is not a continuum."

"No?"

"It's a series of discrete particles—like pearls on a string."

"Yes?"

"Each pearl is a 'Now.' Each 'Now' has its own past and future. But none of them relate to any others. You see? If $a = a_1 + a_2\,ji + \phi ax\,(b_1)$—"

"Never mind the mathematics, Henry."

"It's a form of quantum transfer of energy. Time is emitted in discrete corpuscles or quanta. We can visit each individual quantum and make changes within it, but no change in any one corpuscle affects any other corpuscle. Right?"

"Wrong," I said sorrowfully.

"What d'you mean, 'Wrong'?" he said, angrily gesturing through the cleavage of a passing coed. "You take the trochoid equations and—"

"Wrong," I repeated firmly. "Will you listen to me, Henry?"

"Oh, go ahead," he said.

"Have you noticed that you've become rather insubstantial? Dim? Spectral? Space and time no longer affect you?"

"Yes."

"Henry, I had the misfortune to construct a time machine back in '75."

"So you said. Listen, what about power input? I figure I'm using about 7.3 kilowatts per—"

"Never mind the power input, Henry. On my first trip into

113

the past, I visited the Pleistocene. I was eager to photograph the mastodon, the giant ground sloth, and the saber-toothed tiger. While I was backing up to get a mastodon fully in the field of view at f/6.3 at 1/100 of a second, or on the LVS scale—"

"Never mind the LVS scale," he said.

"While I was backing up, I inadvertently trampled and killed a small Pleistocene insect."

"Aha!" said Hassel.

"I was terrified by the incident. I had visions of returning to my world to find it completely changed as a result of this single death. Imagine my surprise when I returned to my world to find that nothing had changed."

"Oho!" said Hassel.

"I became curious. I went back to the Pleistocene and killed the mastodon. Nothing was changed in 1975. I returned to the Pleistocene and slaughtered the wildlife—still with no effect. I ranged through time, killing and destroying, in an attempt to alter the present."

"Then you did it just like me," Hassel exclaimed. "Odd we didn't run into each other."

"Not odd at all."

"I got Columbus."

"I got Marco Polo."

"I got Napoleon."

"I thought Einstein was more important."

"Mohammed didn't change things much—I expected more from *him*."

"I know. I got him too."

"What do you mean, you got him too?" Hassel demanded.

"I killed him September 16, 599. Old Style."

"Why, I got Mohammed, January 5, 598."

"I believe you."

"But how could you have killed him after I killed him?"

"We both killed him."

"That's impossible."

"My boy," I said, "time is entirely subjective. It's a private matter—a personal experience. There is no such thing as objective time, just as there is no such thing as objective love, or an objective soul."

"Do you mean to say that time travel is impossible? But we've done it."

"To be sure, and many others, for all I know. But we each travel into our own past, and no other person's. There is no universal continuum, Henry. There are only billions of individuals, each with his own continuum; and one continuum cannot affect the other. We're like millions of strands of spaghetti in the same pot. No time traveler can ever meet another time traveler in the past or future. Each of us must travel up and down his own strand alone."

"But we're meeting each other now."

"We're no longer time travelers, Henry. We've become the spaghetti sauce."

"Spaghetti sauce?"

"Yes. You and I can visit any strand we like, because we've destroyed ourselves."

"I don't understand."

"When a man changes the past, he only affects his own past—no one else's. The past is like memory. When you erase a man's memory, you wipe him out, but you don't wipe out anybody else. You and I have erased our past. The individual worlds of the others go on, but we have ceased to exist." I paused significantly.

"What d'you mean, 'ceased to exist'?"

"With each act of destruction we dissolved a little. Now we're all gone. We've committed chronicide. We're ghosts. I hope Mrs. Hassel will be very happy with Mr. Murphy. . . . Now let's go over to the Académie. Ampère is telling a great story about Ludwig Boltzmann."

The Animal Fair
by Robert Bloch

It was dark when the truck dropped Dave off at the deserted freight depot. Dave had to squint to make out the lettering on the weather-faded sign. MEDLEY, OKLAHOMA—POP. 1134.

The trucker said he could probably get another lift on the state highway up past the other end of town, so Dave hit the main drag. And it was a drag.

Nine o'clock of a hot summer evening and Medley was closed for the night. Fred's Eats had locked up, the Jiffy SuperMart had shut down, even Phil's Phill-Up Gas stood deserted. There were no cars parked on the dark street, not even the usual cluster of kids on the corners.

Dave wondered about this, but not for long. In five minutes he covered the length of Main Street and emerged on open fields at the far side, and that's when he saw the lights and heard the music.

They had a carnival going in the little county fairgrounds up ahead—canned music blasting from amplifiers, cars crowding the parking lot, mobs milling across the midway.

Dave wasn't craving this kind of action, but he still had 80 cents in his jeans and he hadn't eaten anything since breakfast. He turned down the side road leading to the fair-grounds.

Like he figured, the carnival was a bummer. One of those little mud shows, traveling by truck; a couple of beat-up rides for the kids and a lot of come-ons for the local yokels. Wheel O' Fortune, Pitch-a-Winner, Take a Chance on a Blanket—that kind of jive. By the time Dave got himself a burger and coffee at one of the stands, he knew the score. A big fat zero.

But not for Medley, Oklahoma—Pop. 1134. The whole damn town was here tonight and probably every red-neck for miles around, shuffling and shoving along the carny street. Dave had to do a little shuffling and shoving himself to get through to the far end of the midway.

And it was there, on the far end, that he saw the small red tent with the tiny platform before it. Hanging limp and listless in the still air, a sun-bleached banner proclaimed the wonders within. CAPTAIN RYDER'S HOLLYWOOD JUNGLE SAFARI, the banner read.

What a Hollywood jungle safari was, Dave didn't know. And the wrinkled cloth posters lining the sides of the entrance weren't much help. A picture of a guy in an explorer's outfit, tangling with a big snake wrapped around his neck—the same joker prying open the jaws of a crocodile—another drawing showing him wrestling a lion. The last poster showed the guy standing next to a cage; inside the cage was a black furry question mark, way over six feet high. The lettering underneath was black and furry, too. WHAT IS IT? SEE THE MIGHTY MONARCH OF THE JUNGLE ALIVE ON THE INSIDE!

Dave didn't know what it was and he cared less. But he'd been bumping along those corduroy roads all day and he was wasted and the noise from the amplifiers here on the midway hurt his ears. At least there was some kind of a show going on

117

inside, and when he saw the open space gaping between the canvas and the ground at the corner of the tent, he stooped and slid under.

The tent was a canvas oven.

Dave could smell oil in the air; on hot summer nights in Oklahoma, you can always smell it. And the crowd in here smelled worse. Bad enough that he was thumbing his way through and couldn't take a bath, but what was their excuse?

The crowd huddled around the base of a portable wooden stage at the rear of the tent, listening to a pitch from Captain Ryder. At least that's who Dave figured it was, even though the character with the phony safari hat and the dirty white riding breeches didn't look much like his pictures on the banners. He was handing out a spiel in one of those hoarse, gravelly voices that carry without a microphone—some hype about being a Hollywood stunt man and African explorer—and there wasn't a snake or a crocodile or a lion anywhere in sight.

The two-bit hamburger began churning up a storm in Dave's guts, and between the body heat and the smells, he'd just about had it in here. He started to turn and push his way through the mob when the man up on the stage thumped the boards with his cane.

"And now, friends, if you'll gather round a little closer—"

The crowd swept forward in unison, like the straws of a giant broom, and Dave found himself pressed right up against the edge of the square-shaped, canvas-covered pit beside the end of the platform. He couldn't get through now if he tried; all the red-necks were bunched together, waiting.

Dave waited, too, but he stopped listening to the voice on the platform. All that jive about Darkest Africa was a put-on. Maybe these clowns went for it, but Dave wasn't buying a word. He just hoped the old guy would hurry and get the show over with; all he wanted now was out of here.

Captain Ryder tapped the canvas covering the pit with his cane, and his harsh tones rose. The heat made Dave yawn loudly, but some of the phrases filtered through.

"—about to see here tonight the world's most ferocious monster—captured at deadly peril to life and limb—"

Dave shook his head. He knew what was in the pit. Some crummy animal picked up secondhand from a circus, maybe a scroungy hyena. And two to one it wasn't even alive, just stuffed. Big deal.

Captain Ryder lifted the canvas cover and pulled it back behind the pit. He flourished his cane.

"Behold—the lord of the jungle!"

The crowd pressed, pushed, peered over the rim of the pit.

The crowd gasped.

And Dave, pressing and peering with the rest, stared at the creature blinking up at him from the bottom of the pit.

It was a live, full-grown gorilla.

The monster squatted on a heap of straw, its huge forearms secured to steel stakes by lengths of heavy chain. It gaped upward at the rim of faces, moving its great, gray head slowly from side to side, the yellow-fanged mouth open and the massive jaws set in a vacant grimace. Only the little rheumy, red-rimmed eyes held a hint of expression—enough to tell Dave, who had never seen a gorilla before, that this animal was sick.

The matted straw at the base of the pit was wet and stained; in one corner, a battered tin plate rested untouched, its surface covered with a soggy slop of shredded carrots, okra and turnip greens floating in an oily scum beneath a cloud of buzzing blowflies. In the stifling heat of the tent, the acrid odor rising from the pit was almost overwhelming.

Dave felt his stomach muscles constrict. He tried to force his attention back to Captain Ryder. The old guy was step-

119

ping offstage now, moving behind the pit and reaching down into it with his cane.

"Nothing to be afraid of, folks; as you can see, he's perfectly harmless, aren't you, Bobo?"

The gorilla whimpered, huddling back against the soiled straw to avoid the prodding cane. But the chains confined movement, and the cane began to dig its tip into the beast's shaggy shoulders.

"And now Bobo's going to do a little dance for the folks—right?" The gorilla whimpered again, but the point of the cane jabbed deeply and the rasping voice firmed in command.

"Up, Bobo—up!"

The creature lumbered to its haunches. As the cane rose and fell about its shoulders, the bulky body began to sway. The crowd oohed and aahed and snickered.

"That's it! Dance for the people, Bobo—dance!"

A swarm of flies spiraled upward to swirl about the furry form shimmering in the heat. Dave saw the sick beast shuffle, moving to and fro, and to and fro. Then his stomach was moving in responsive rhythm and he had to shut his eyes as he turned and fought his way blindly through the murmuring mob.

"Hey—watch where the hell ya goin', fella."

Dave got out of the tent just in time.

Getting rid of the hamburger helped, and getting away from the carnival grounds helped, too, but not enough. As Dave moved up the road between the open fields, he felt the nausea return. The oily air made him dizzy, and he knew he'd have to lie down for a minute. He dropped into the ditch beside the road, shielded behind a clump of weeds, and closed his eyes to stop the whirling sensation. Only for a minute—

The dizziness went away, but behind his closed eyes he could still see the gorilla, still see the expressionless face and the all-too-expressive eyes. Eyes peering up from the pile of dirty straw in the pit, eyes clouding with pain and hopeless resignation as the chains clanked and the cane flicked across the hairy shoulders.

Ought to be a law, Dave thought. There must be some kind of law to stop it, treating a poor dumb animal like that. And the old guy, Captain Ryder—there ought to be a law for an animal like him, too.

Ah, to hell with it. Better shut it out of his mind now, get some rest. Another couple of minutes wouldn't hurt.

It was the thunder that finally woke him. The thunder jerked him into awareness, and then he felt the warm, heavy drops pelting his head and face.

Dave rose and the wind swept over him, whistling across the fields. He must have been asleep for hours, because everything was pitch black, and when he glanced behind him, the lights of the carnival were gone.

For an instant, the sky turned silver and he could see the rain pour down; then the thunder came again, giving him the message. This wasn't just a summer shower, it was a real storm. Another minute and he was going to be soaking wet. By the time he got up to the state highway, he could drown, and even if he made it there, chances for a lift looked bad. Nobody traveled in this weather. Maybe he could find some kind of shelter, he thought.

Dave zipped up his jacket, pulled the collar around his neck. It didn't help, and neither did walking up the road, but he might as well get going. The wind was at his back, and that helped a little, but moving against the rain was like walking through a wall of water.

Another flicker of lightning, another rumble of thunder. And then the flickering and the rumbling merged and held steady; suddenly the light grew brighter and a sound rose over the hiss of wind and rain.

Dave glanced back over his shoulder and saw the source—the headlights and engine of a truck coming along the road from behind him. As it moved closer, Dave realized it wasn't a truck; it was a camper, one of those two-decker jobs with a driver's cab up front.

Right now, he didn't give a damn what it was, as long as it stopped and picked him up. Before the camper came alongside him, Dave stepped out, waving his arms.

The camper slowed, halted. The shadow in the cab leaned over from behind the wheel and a hand pushed the window vent open on the passenger side. "Want a lift, buddy? Get in."

The door swung open and Dave climbed up into the cab. He slid onto the seat and pulled the door shut behind him. The camper started to move again.

"Shut the window," the driver said. "Rain's blowing in."

Dave closed it, then wished he hadn't. The air inside the cab was heavy with odors—not just perspiration but something else. Dave recognized the smell even before the driver produced the bottle from his jacket pocket.

"Want a slug? Fresh corn likker. Tastes like hell, but it's better 'n nothing."

"No, thanks."

"Suit yourself." The bottle tilted and gurgled; lightning flared across the roadway ahead, glinting against the glass of the windshield, the glass of the upturned bottle. In its momentary glare Dave caught a glimpse of the driver's face, and the flash of lightning brought a flash of recognition. The driver was Captain Ryder.

Thunder growled, prowling the sky, and the heavy camper turned onto the slick, rain-swept surface of the state highway.

"What's the matter, you deaf or something? I asked you where you're heading."

Dave came to with a start. "Oklahoma City," he said.

"You hit the jackpot. That's where I'm going."

Some jackpot. Dave had been thinking about the old guy, remembering the gorilla in the pit. He hated this bastard's guts, and the idea of riding with him all the way to Oklahoma City made his stomach churn again. On the other hand, walking along in a storm in the middle of the prairie was no great stomach soother, so what the hell?

The camper lurched and Ryder fought the wheel. "Boy— sure is a cutter! Get these things often around here?"

"I wouldn't know," Dave said. "This is my first time through. I'm meeting a friend in Oklahoma City. We figure on driving out to Hollywood together."

"Hollywood?" The hoarse voice deepened. "That god-damn place!"

"But don't you come from there?"

Ryder glanced up quickly, and lightning flickered across his sudden frown. Seeing him this close, Dave realized he wasn't so old; something besides time had shaped that scowl, etched the bitter lines around eyes and mouth.

"Who told you that?" Ryder said.

"I was at the carnival tonight. I saw your show."

Ryder grunted, and his eyes tracked the road ahead through the twin pendulums of the windshield wipers. "Pretty lousy, huh?"

Dave began to nod, then caught himself. No sense start-ing anything. "That gorilla of yours looked like it might be sick."

"Bobo? He's all right. Just the weather. We open up North, he'll be fine." Ryder nodded in the direction of the camper bulking behind him. "Haven't heard a peep out of him since we started."

"He's traveling with you?"

"Whaddya think, I ship him airmail?" A hand rose from the wheel, gesturing. "This camper's built special. I got the upstairs, he's down below. I keep the back open so's he gets some air, but no problem—I got it all barred. Take a look through that window behind you."

Dave turned and peered through the wire-meshed window at the rear of the cab. He could see the lighted interior of the camper's upper level, neatly and normally outfitted for occupancy. Shifting his gaze, he stared into the darkness below. Lashed securely to the side walls were the tent, the platform boards, the banners and the rigging; the floor space between them was covered with straw, heaped into a sort of nest. Crouched against the barred opening at the far end was the black bulk of the gorilla, back turned as it faced the road to the rear, intent on the roaring rain. The camper went into a skid for a moment and the beast twitched, jerking its head around so that Dave caught a glimpse of its glazed eyes. It seemed to whimper softly, but because of the thunder, Dave couldn't be sure.

"Snug as a bug," Ryder said. "And so are we." He had the bottle out again, deftly uncorking it with one hand. "Sure you don't want a belt?"

"I'll pass," Dave said.

The bottle raised, then paused. "Hey, wait a minute." Ryder was scowling at him again. "You're not on something else, are you, buddy?"

"Drugs?" Dave shook his head. "Not me."

"Good thing you're not." The bottle tilted, lowered again as Ryder corked it. "I hate that crap. Drugs. Drugs and hippies. Hollywood's full of both. You take my advice, you keep away from there. No place for a kid, not anymore." He belched loudly, started to put the bottle into his jacket pocket, then uncorked it again.

Dave saw that the captain was on his way to getting loaded. Best thing to do would be to keep him talking, take his mind off the bottle before he knocked the camper off the road.

"No kidding, were you really a Hollywood stunt man?" Dave said.

"Sure, one of the best. But that was back in the old days, before the place went to hell. Worked for all the majors—trick riding, fancy falls, doubling fight scenes, the works. You ask anybody who knows, they'll tell you old Cap Ryder was right up there with Yakima Canutt, maybe even better." The voice rasped on, harsh and proud. "Seven-fifty a day, that's what I drew. Seven hundred and fifty, every day I worked. And I worked a lot."

"I didn't know they paid that kind of dough," Dave said.

"You got to remember one thing. I wasn't just taking falls in the long shots. When they hired Cap Ryder, they knew they were getting some fancy talent. Not many stunt men can handle animals. You ever see any of those old jungle pictures on television—Tarzan movies, stuff like that? Well, in over half of 'em, I'm the guy handling the cats. Lions, leopards, tigers, you name it."

"Sounds exciting."

"Sure, if you like hospitals. In one shot, I wrestled a black panther, like to rip my arm clean off. Seven-fifty sounds like a lot of loot, but you should have seen what I laid out in medical bills. Not to mention what I paid for costumes and extras. Like the lionskins and the apesuit—"

"I don't get it." Dave frowned. "Costumes?"

"Sometimes they need an action shot close up and the star's face has to be in it. Well, of course they can't use a real animal, so if it was a fight scene with a lion or whatever, that's where I came in handy—I doubled for the animal. Would you believe it, three grand I laid out for a lousy

125

monkey suit alone! But it paid off. You should have seen the big pad I had overlooking Laurel Canyon. Four bedrooms, three-car garage, tennis court, swimming pool, sauna, everything you can think of. Melissa loved it—"

"Melissa?"

Ryder shook his head. "What'm I talking about? You don't want to hear any of that crud about the good old days. All water over the dam."

The mention of water evidently reminded him of thirst, because he reached for the bottle again. And this time, when he tilted it, it gurgled its last. Ryder cranked the window down and flung the bottle out into the rain.

"All gone," he muttered. "Finished. No more bottle. No more house. No more Melissa."

"Who was she?" Dave said.

"You really want to know?" Ryder jerked his thumb toward the windshield. Dave followed the gesture, puzzled, until he raised his glance to the roof of the cab. There, fastened directly above the rearview mirror, was a small picture frame. Staring out of it was the face of a girl; blond hair, nice features and the kind of smile you see in the pages of high school annuals.

"My niece," Ryder told him. "Sixteen. But I took her when she was only five, right after my sister died. Took her and raised her for eleven years. Raised her right, too. Let me tell you, that girl never lacked for anything. Whatever she wanted, whatever she needed, she got. The trips we took together—the good times we had—hell, I guess it sounds silly, but you'd be surprised what a kick you can get out of seeing a kid have fun. And smart? President of the junior class at Brixley—that's the name of the private school I put her in; best in town; half the stars sent their own daughters there. And that's what she was to me, just like my own flesh-and-blood daughter. So go figure it. How it happened

126

I'll never know." Ryder blinked at the road ahead, forcing his eyes into focus.

"How what happened?" Dave asked.

"The hippies. The goddamn sons-a-bitching hippies."

Dave noticed that Ryder's eyes were suddenly alert amid the network of ugly wrinkles.

"Don't ask me where she met the bastards," Ryder continued. "I thought I was guarding her from all that, but those lousy freaks are all over the place. She must've run into them through one of her friends at school—Christ knows, you see plenty of weirdos even in Bel Air. But you got to remember, she was just sixteen, and how could she guess what she was getting into? I suppose at that age, an older guy with a beard and a Fender guitar and a souped-up cycle looks pretty exciting.

"Anyhow, they got to her one night when I was away on location. Maybe she invited them over to the house, maybe they just showed up and she asked them in. Four of 'em, all stoned out of their skulls. Dude, that was the oldest one's name. He was like the leader, and it was his idea from the start. Everybody knew that she never smoked grass or fooled around with drugs, so I guess he got the idea of pulling a fast one. Must have asked her to serve something to drink, and then he probably slipped the stuff into her glass. Enough to finish off a bull elephant, the coroner said."

"You mean it killed her?"

"Not right away. I wish to Christ it had." Ryder turned, his face working, and Dave had to strain to hear his voice through the rush of rain.

"According to the coroner, she must have lived for at least an hour. Long enough for them to take turns—Dude and the three others. Long enough after that for them to get the idea.

"They were in my den, and I had the place all fixed up like a kind of trophy room—animal skins all over the wall, native

127

drums, voodoo masks, stuff I'd picked up on my trips. And here were these four freaks, spaced out, and the kid, blowing her mind. One of the bastards took down a drum and started beating on it. Another got hold of a mask and started hopping around like a witch doctor. And Dude—it was Dude, all right, I know it for sure—he and the other creep pulled the lionskin off the wall and draped it over Melissa. Because this was a trip and they were playing Africa. Great White Hunter. Me Tarzan, you Jane.

"By this time, Melissa couldn't even stand up anymore. Dude got her down on her hands and knees and she just wobbled there. And then—that dirty rotten son of a bitch— he pulled down the drapery cords and tied the lionskin over her head and shoulders. And he took a spear down from the wall, one of the Masai spears, and he was going to jab her in the ribs with it.

"That's what I saw when I went in. Dude, the big stud, standing over Melissa with that spear.

"He didn't stand long. One look at me and the fun was over. I think he threw the spear before he ran, but I can't remember. I can't remember anything about the next couple of minutes. They said I broke one freak's collarbone, and the creep in the mask had a concussion from where his head hit the wall. The third one was almost dead by the time the squad arrived and pried my fingers loose from his neck. As it was, they were too late to save him.

"And they were too late for Melissa. She just lay there under that dirty lionskin—that's the part I do remember, the part I wish I could forget—"

"You killed a kid?" Dave said.

Ryder shook his head. "I killed an animal. That's what I told them at the trial. When an animal goes vicious, you got a right. The judge said one to five, but I was out in a little over two years." He glanced at Dave. "Ever been inside?"

"No. How is it—rough?"

"You can say that again. Rough as a cob." Ryder's stomach rumbled. "I went in pretty feisty, so they put me down in solitary for a while, and that didn't help. You sit there in the dark and you start thinking. Here am I, used to traveling all over the world, penned up in a little cage like an animal. And one of those animals who killed Melissa is running free. One was dead, of course, and the two others I tangled with had maybe learned their lesson. But the big one, the one who started it all, he was loose. Cops never did catch up with him, and they weren't about to waste any more time trying, now that the trial was over.

"I thought a lot about Dude. That was the big one's name, or did I tell you?" Ryder's head swayed with the movement of the cab, and in the dim light he seemed well on his way to being smashed. But his driving was still steady, and Dave could keep him awake if he could keep him talking.

"So, what happened?" Dave asked.

"Mostly, I thought about what I was going to do to Dude once I got out. Finding him would be tricky, but I knew I could do it—hell, I spent years in Africa, tracking animals. And I intended to hunt this one down."

"Then it's true about you being an explorer?" Dave asked.

"Animal trapper," Ryder said. "Kenya, Uganda, Nigeria—this was before Hollywood—and I saw it all. Things these young punks today never dreamed of. Why, they were dancing and drumming and drugging over there before the first hippie crawled out from under his rock, and let me tell you, they know how to do this stuff for real.

"Like when this Dude tied the lionskin on Melissa, he was just freaked out, playing games. He should have seen what some of those witch doctors can do.

"First, they steal themselves a girl, sometimes a young boy, but let's say a girl because of Melissa. And they shut her up in a cave—a cave with a low ceiling, so she can't stand up, has to go on all fours. They put her on drugs right away, heavy doses, enough to keep her out for a long time. And when she wakes up, her hands and feet have been operated on, so they can be fitted with claws. Lion claws. And they've sewed her into a lionskin. Not just put it over her—it's sewed on completely and can't be removed.

"You just think about what it's like. She's inside this lionskin, shut away in a cave, doped up, doesn't know where she is or what's going on. And they keep her that way. Feed her nothing but raw meat. She's all alone in the dark, smelling that damn lion smell, nobody talking to her and nobody for her to talk to. Then pretty soon they come in and break some bones in her throat, her larynx, and all she can do is whine and growl. Whine and growl and move around on all fours.

"You know what happens, boy? You know what happens to someone like that? They go crazy. And after a while, they get to believing they really are a lion. The next step is for the witch doctor to take them out and train them to kill, but that's another story."

Dave glanced up quickly. "You're putting me on."

"It's all there in the government reports. Maybe the jets go into Nairobi airport now, but back in the bush, things haven't changed. Like I say, some of these people know more about drugs than any hippie ever will. Especially a stupid animal like Dude."

"What happened after you got out?" Dave said. "Did you ever catch up with him?"

Ryder shook his head.

"But I thought you said you had it all planned."

"Fella gets a lot of weird ideas in solitary. In a way it's pretty much like being shut up in one of those caves. Come to think of it, that's what first reminded me—"

"Of what?"

"Nothing." Ryder gestured hastily. "Forget it. That's what *I* did. When I got out, I figured that was the best way. Forgive and forget."

"You didn't even try to find Dude?"

Ryder frowned. "I told you, I had other things to think about. Like being washed up in the business, losing the house, the furniture, everything. Also, I had a drinking problem. But you don't want to hear about that. Anyway, I ended up with the carny, and there's nothing more to tell."

Lightning streaked across the sky and thunder rolled in its wake. Dave turned his head, glancing back through the wire-meshed window. The gorilla was still hunched at the far end, peering through the bars into the night beyond. Dave stared at him for a long moment, not really wanting to stop, because then he knew he'd have to ask the question.

The Jar
by Ray Bradbury

It was one of those things they keep in a jar in the tent of a sideshow on the outskirts of a little, drowsy town. One of those pale things drifting in alcohol plasma, forever dreaming and circling, with its peeled, dead eyes staring out at you and never seeing you. It went with the noiselessness of late night, and only the crickets chirping, the frogs sobbing off in the moist swampland. One of those things in a big jar that makes your stomach jump as it does when you see a preserved arm in a laboratory vat.

Charlie stared back at it for a long time.

A long time, his big, raw hands, hairy on the roofs of them, clenching the rope that kept back curious people. He had paid his dime and now he stared.

It was getting late. The merry-go-round drowsed down to a lazy mechanical tinkle. Tent-peggers back of a canvas smoked and cursed over a poker game. Lights switched out, putting a summer gloom over the carnival. People streamed homeward in cliques and queues. Somewhere, a radio flared up, then cut, leaving the Louisiana sky wide and silent with stars.

There was nothing in the world for Charlie but that pale

thing sealed in its universe of serum. Charlie's loose mouth hung open in a pink weal, teeth showing; his eyes were puzzled, admiring, wondering.

Someone walked in the shadows behind him, small beside Charlie's gaunt tallness. "Oh," said the shadow, coming into the light-bulb glare. "You still here, bud?"

"Yeah," said Charlie, like a man in his sleep.

The carny-boss appreciated Charlie's curiosity. He nodded at his old acquaintance in the jar. "Everybody likes it—in a peculiar kinda way, I mean."

Charlie rubbed his long jaw-bone. "You—uh—ever consider selling it?"

The carny-boss's eyes dilated, then closed. He snorted. "Naw. It brings customers. They like seeing stuff like that. Sure."

Charlie made a disappointed "Oh."

"Well," considered the carny-boss, "if a guy had money, maybe——"

"How much money?"

"If a guy had——" the carny-boss estimated, counting fingers, watching Charlie as he tacked it out one finger after another. "If a guy had three, four, say—maybe seven or eight——"

Charlie nodded with each motion, expectantly. Seeing this, the carny-boss raised his total, "—maybe ten dollars, or maybe fifteen——"

Charlie scowled, worried. The carny-boss retreated. "Say a guy has *twelve* dollars——" Charlie grinned. "Why he could buy that thing in that jar," concluded the carny-boss.

"Funny thing," said Charlie, "I got just twelve bucks in my denims. And I been reckoning how looked-up-to I'd be back down at Wilder's Hollow if I brung home something like this to set on my shelf over the table. The folks would sure look up to me then, I bet."

"*Well*, now, listen here———" said the carny-boss.

The sale was completed with the jar put on the back seat of Charlie's wagon. The horse skittered his hoofs when he saw the jar, and whinnied.

The carny-boss glanced up with an expression almost of relief. "I was tired of seeing that damn thing around, anyway. Don't thank me. Lately I been thinking things about it, funny things———but, hell, I'm a big-mouthed so-and-so. S'long, farmer!"

Charlie drove off. The naked blue light bulbs withdrew like dying stars; the open, dark country night of Louisiana swept in around wagon and horse. There was just Charlie, the horse timing his gray hoofs, and the crickets.

And the jar behind the high seat.

It sloshed back and forth, back and forth. Sloshed wet. And the cold gray thing drowsily slumped against the glass, looking out, looking out, but seeing nothing, nothing.

Charlie leaned back to pet the lid. Smelling of strange liquor, his hand returned, changed and cold and trembling, excited. *Yes, sir!* he thought to himself, *Yes, sir!*

Slosh, slosh, slosh. . . .

In the Hollow, numerous grass-green and blood-red lanterns tossed dusty light over men huddled, murmuring, spitting, sitting on General Store property.

They knew the creak-bumble of Charlie's wagon and did not shift their raw, drab-haired skulls as he rocked to a halt. Their cigars were glowworms; their voices were frog mutterings on summer nights.

Charlie leaned down eagerly. "Hi, Clem! Hi, Milt!"

"Lo, Charlie. Lo, Charlie," they murmured. The political conflict continued. Charlie cut it down the seam:

"I got somethin' here. I got somethin' you might wanna see!"

Tom Carmody's eyes glinted, green in the lamplight, from

the General Store porch. It seemed to Charlie that Tom Carmody was forever installed under porches in shadow, or under trees in shadow, or if in a room, then in the farthest niche, shining his eyes out at you from the dark. You never knew what his face was doing, and his eyes were always funning you. And every time they looked at you, they laughed a different way.

"You ain't got nothin' we wants to see, baby-doll."

Charlie made a fist and looked at it. "Somethin' in a jar," he went on. "Looks kine a like a brain, kine a like a pickled jellyfish, kine a like—well, come see yourself!"

Someone snicked a cigar into a fall of pink ash and ambled over to look. Charlie grandly elevated the jar lid, and in the uncertain lantern light the man's face changed. "Hey, now, what in hell *is* this——?"

It was the first thaw of the evening. Others shifted lazily upright, leaned forward; gravity pulled them into walking. They made no effort, except to put one shoe before the other to keep from collapsing upon their unusual faces. They circled the jar and contents. And Charlie, for the first time in his life, seized on some hidden strategy and crashed the glass lid shut.

"You want to see more, drop aroun' my house! It'll be there," he declared generously.

Tom Carmody spat from out his porch eyrie. "Ha!"

"Lemme see that again!" cried Gramps Medknowe. "Is it a octopus?"

Charlie flapped the reins; the horse stumbled into action.

"Come on aroun'! You're welcome!"

"What'll your wife say?"

"She'll kick the tar off'n our heels!"

But Charlie and wagon were gone over the hill. The men stood, all of them, chewing their tongues, squinting up the road in the dark. Tom Carmody swore softly from the porch. . . .

Charlie climbed the steps of his shack and carried the jar to its throne in the living room, thinking that from now on this lean-to would be a palace, with an "emperor"—that was the word! "emperor"—all cold and white and quiet drifting in his private pool, raised, elevated upon a shelf over a ramshackle table.

The jar, as he watched, burnt off the cold mist that hung over this place on the rim of the swamp.

"What you got there?"

Thedy's thin soprano turned him from his awe. She stood in the bedroom door, glaring out, her thin body clothed in faded blue gingham, her hair drawn to a drab knot behind red ears. Her eyes were faded like the gingham. "Well," she repeated, "what is it?"

"What's it look like to you, Thedy?"

She took a thin step forward, making a slow, indolent pendulum of hips, her eyes intent upon the jar, her lips drawn back to show feline milk teeth.

The dead pale thing hung in its serum.

Thedy snapped a dull-blue glance at Charlie, then back to the jar, once more at Charlie, once more to the jar; then she whirled quickly.

"It—it looks—looks just like *you*, Charlie!" she cried.

The bedroom door slammed.

The reverberation did not disturb the jar's contents. But Charlie stood there, longing after his wife, heart pounding frantically. Much later, when his heart slowed, he talked to the thing in the jar.

"I work the bottom land to the butt-bone every year, and she grabs the money and runs off down home visitin' her folks nine weeks at a stretch. I can't keep hold of her. Her and the men from the store, they make fun of me. I can't help it if I don't know a way to hold onto her! Damn, but I *try!*"

Philosophically, the contents of the jar gave no advice.

"Charlie?"

Someone stood in the front-yard door.

Charlie turned, startled, then broke out a grin.

It was some of the men from the General Store.

"Uh—Charlie—we—we thought—well—we came up to have a look at that—stuff—you got in that there jar——"

July passed warm, and it was August.

For the first time in years, Charlie was happy as tall corn growing after a drought. It was gratifying of an evening to hear boots shushing through the tall grass, the sound of men spitting into the ditch prior to setting foot on the porch, the sound of heavy bodies creaking the boards, and the groan of the house as yet another shoulder leaned against its frame door and another voice said, as a hairy wrist wiped a mouth clean:

"Kin I come in?"

With elaborate casualness, Charlie'd invite the arrivals in. There'd be chairs, soapboxes for all, or at least carpets to squat on. And by the time crickets were itching their legs into a summertime humming and frogs were throat-swollen like ladies with goiters shouting in the great night, the room would be full to bursting with people from all the bottom lands.

At first nobody would say anything. The first half-hour of such an evening, while people came in and got settled, was spent in carefully rolling cigarettes. Putting tobacco neatly into the rut of brown paper, loading it, tamping it, as they loaded and tamped and rolled their thoughts and fears and amazement for the evening. It gave them time to think. You could see their brains working behind their eyes as they fingered the cigarettes into smoking order.

It was kind of a rude church gathering. They sat, squatted, leaned on plaster walls; and one by one, with reverent awe, they stared at the jar upon its shelf.

They wouldn't stare sudden-like. No, they kind of did it

137

slow, casual, as if they were glancing around the room—
letting their eyes fumble over just *any* old object that happened into their consciousness.

And—just by accident, of course—the focus of their
wandering eyes would occur always at the same place. After
a while all eyes in the room would be fastened to it, like pins
stuck in some incredible pincushion. And the only sound
would be someone sucking a corncob. Or the children's
barefooted scurry on the porch planks outside. Maybe some
woman's voice would come, "You kids git away, now! Git!"
And with a giggle like soft, quick water, the bare feet would
rush off to scare the bullfrogs.

Charlie would be up front, naturally, on his rocking chair,
a plaid pillow under his lean rump, rocking slow, enjoying
the fame and looked-up-to-ness that came with keeping the
jar.

Thedy, she'd be seen way back of the room with the
womenfolk in a bunch, all gray and quiet, abiding their
men.

Thedy looked like she was ripe for jealous screaming. But
she said nothing, just watched men tromp into her living
room and sit at the feet of Charlie, staring at this here Holy
Grail-like thing, and her lips were set cold and hard, and she
spoke not a civil word to anybody.

After a period of proper silence, someone—maybe old
Gramps Medknowe from Crick Road—would clear the
phlegm from a deep cave somewhere inside himself, lean
forward, blinking, wet his lips, maybe, and there'd be a
curious tremble in his calloused fingers.

This would cue everyone to get ready for the talking to
come. Ears were primed. People settled like sows in the
warm mud after a rain.

Gramps looked a long while, measured his lips with a
lizard tongue, then settled back and said, like always, in a
high, thin old-man's tenor:

"Wonder what it is? Wonder if it's a he or a she or just a plain old *it?* Sometimes I wake up nights, twist on my corn-mattin', think about that jar settin' here in the long dark. Think about it hangin' in liquid, peaceful and pale like an animal oyster. Sometimes I wake Maw and we both think on it. . . ."

While talking, Gramps moved his fingers in a quavering pantomime. Everybody watched his thick thumb weave, and the other heavy-nailed fingers undulate.

". . . we both lay there, thinkin'. And we shivers. Maybe a hot night, trees sweatin', mosquitoes too hot to fly, but we shivers jest the same, and turn over, tryin' to sleep. . . ."

Gramps lapsed back into silence, as if his speech was enough from him; let some other voice talk the wonder, awe, and strangeness.

Juke Marmer, from Willow Sump, wiped sweat off his palms on the round of his knees and softly said:

"I remember when I was a runnel-nosed kid. We had a cat who was all the time makin' kittens. Lordamighty, she'd a litter any time she jumped around and skipped a fence——" Juke spoke in a kind of holy softness, benevolent. "Well, we give the kittens away, but when this one particular litter busted out, everybody within walkin' distance had one-two our cats by gift, already.

"So Ma busied on the back porch with a big two-gallon glass jar, fillin' it to the top with water. Ma said, 'Juke, you drown them kittens!' I 'member I stood there; the kittens mewed, runnin' 'round, blind, small, helpless, and funny—just beginnin' to get their eyes open. I looked at Ma; I said, 'Not *me*, Ma! *You* do it!' But Ma turned pale and said it had to be done and I was the only one handy. And she went off to stir gravy and fix chicken. I—I picked up one—kitten. I held it. It was warm. It made a mewin' sound. I felt like runnin' away, not ever comin' back."

Juke nodded his head now, eyes bright, young, seeing

into the past, making it new, shaping it with words, smoothing it with his tongue.

"I dropped the kitten in the water. The kitten closed his eyes, opened his mouth, tryin' for air. I 'member how the little white fangs showed, the pink tongue came out, and bubbles with it, in a line to the top of the water!

"I know to this day the way that kitten floated after it was all over, driftin' aroun', slow and not worryin', lookin' out at me, not condemnin' me for what I done. But not likin' me, neither. Ahhhh. . . ."

Hearts jumped quick. Eyes swiveled from Juke to the shelved jar, back down, up again apprehensively.

A pause.

Jahdoo, the black man from Heron Swamp, tossed his ivory eyeballs, like a dusky juggler, in his head. His dark knuckles knotted and flexed—grasshoppers alive.

"You know what that is? You know, you *know?* I tells you. That be the center of Life, sure 'nuff! Lord believe me, it so!"

Swaying in a tree-like rhythm, Jahdoo was blown by a swamp wind no one could see, hear or feel, save himself. His eyeballs went around again, as if cut free to wander. His voice needled a dark thread pattern, picking up each person by the lobes of ears and sewing them into one unbreathing design:

"From that, lyin' back in the Middibamboo Sump, all sort o' thing crawl. It put out hand, it put out feet, it put out tongue an' horn an' it grow. Little bitty amoeba, perhap. Then a frog with a bulge-throat fit ta bust! Yah!" He cracked knuckles. "It slobber on up to its gummy joints and it—it AM HUMAN! That am the center of creation! That am Middibamboo Mama, from which we all come ten thousand year ago. Believe it!"

"Ten thousand year ago!" whispered Granny Carnation.

"It am old! Looky it! It donn worra no more. It know betta.

140

It hang like pork chop in fryin' fat. It got eye to see with, but it donn blink 'em, they donn look fretted, does they? No, man! It know betta. It know that we done come *from* it, and we is goin' back *to* it."

"What color eyes it got?"

"Gray."

"Naw, *green!*"

"What color hair? Brown?"

"Black!"

"Red!"

"No, *gray!*"

Then, Charlie would give his drawling opinion. Some nights he'd say the same thing, some nights not. It didn't matter. When you said the same thing night after night in the deep summer, it always sounded different. The crickets changed it. The frogs changed it. The thing in the jar changed it. Charlie said:

"What if an old man went back into the swamp, or maybe a young kid, and wandered aroun' for years and years lost in all that drippin', on the trails and gullies, in them old wet ravines in the nights, skin a turnin' pale, and makin' cold and shrivelin' up? Bein' away from the sun, he'd keep witherin' away up and up and finally sink into a muck-hole and lay in a kind of—scum—like the maggot 'skeeters sleepin' in sump-water. Why, why—for all we can tell, this might be someone we *know!* Someone we passed words with once on a time. For all we know———"

A hissing from among the womenfolk back in the shadow. One woman standing, eyes shining black, fumbled for words. Her name was Mrs. Tridden, and she murmured:

"Lots of little kids run stark naked to the swamp ever' year. They runs around and never comes back. I almost got lost maself. I—I lost my little boy, Foley, that way. You—you DON'T SUPPOSE! ! !"

Breath was snatched through nostrils, constricted, tightened. Mouths turned down at corners, bent by hard, clinching muscle. Heads turned on celery-stalk necks, and eyes read her horror and hope. It was in Mrs. Tridden's body, wire-taut, holding to the wall back of her with straight fingers stiff.

"My baby," she whispered. She breathed it out. "My baby. My Foley. Foley! Foley, is that you? Foley! Foley, tell me, baby, is that YOU?"

Everybody held his breath, turning to see the jar.

The thing in the jar said nothing. It just stared blind-white out upon the multitude. And deep in rawboned bodies a secret fear juice ran like a spring thaw, and their resolute calmness and belief and easy humbleness was gnawed and eaten by that juice and melted away in a torrent! Someone screamed.

"It moved!"

"No, no, it didn' move. Just your eyes playin' tricks!"

"Hones' ta God!" cried Juke. "I saw it shift slow like a dead kitten!"

"Hush up, now. It's been dead a long, long time. Maybe since before you was born!"

"He made a sign!" screamed Mrs. Tridden. "That's my Foley! My baby you got there! Three-year-old he was! My baby lost and gone in the swamp!"

The sobbing broke from her.

"Now, Mrs. Tridden. There now. Set yourself down; stop shakin'. Ain't no more your child'n mine. There, there."

One of the womenfolk held her and faded out the sobbing into jerked breathing and a fluttering of her lips in butterfly quickness as the breath stroked over them, afraid.

When all was quiet again, Granny Carnation, with a withered pink flower in her shoulder-length gray hair, sucked the pipe in her trap mouth and talked around it, shaking her head to make the hair dance in the light:

"All this talkin' and shovin' words. Like as not we'll never find out, never know what it is. Like as not if we found out we wouldn't *want* to know. It's like magic tricks magicians do at shows. Once you find the fake, ain't no more fun'n the innards of a jackbob. We come collectin' around here every ten nights or so, talkin', social-like, with somethin', always somethin', to talk about. Stands to reason if we spied out what the damn thing is, there'd be nothin' to chew about, so there!"

"Well, damn it to hell!" rumbled a bull voice. "I don't think it's nothin'!"

Tom Carmody.

Tom Carmody standing, as always, in shadow. Out on the porch, just his eyes staring in, his lips laughing at you dimly, mocking. His laughter got inside Charlie like a hornet sting. Thedy had put him up to it. Thedy was trying to kill Charlie's new life, she was!

"Nothin'," repeated Carmody harshly, "in that jar but a bunch of old jellyfish from Sea Cove, a rottin' and stinkin' fit to whelp!"

"You mightn't be jealous, Cousin Carmody?" asked Charlie, slow.

"Haw!" snorted Carmody. "I just come aroun' ta watch you dumb fools jaw about nothin'. You notice I never set foot inside or took part. I'm goin' home right now. Anybody wanna come along with me?"

He got no offer of company. He laughed again, as if this were a bigger joke, how so many people could be so far gone, and Thedy was raking her palms with her fingernails away back in a corner of the room. Charlie saw her mouth twitch and was cold and could not speak.

Carmody, still laughing, rapped off the porch with his

high-heeled boots, and the sound of crickets took him away.

Granny Carnation gummed her pipe. "Like I was sayin' before the storm: that thing on the shelf, why couldn't it be sort of—all things? Lots of things. All kinds of life—death—I don't know. Mix rain and sun and muck and jelly, all that together. Grass and snakes and children and mist and all the nights and days in the dead canebrake. Why's it have to be *one* thing? Maybe it's *lots*."

And the talking ran soft for another hour, and Thedy slipped away into the night on the track of Tom Carmody, and Charlie began to sweat. They were up to something, those two. They were planning something. Charlie sweated warm all the rest of the evening. . . .

The meeting broke up late, and Charlie bedded down with mixed emotions. The meeting had gone off well, but what about Thedy and Tom?

Very late, with certain star coveys shuttled down the sky marking the time as after midnight, Charlie heard the shushing of the tall grass parted by her penduluming hips. Her heels tacked soft across the porch, into the house, into the bedroom.

She lay soundlessly in bed, cat eyes staring at him. He couldn't see them, but he could feel them staring.

"Charlie?"

He waited.

Then he said, "I'm awake."

Then she waited.

"Charlie?"

"What?"

"Bet you don't know where I been; bet you don't know where I been." It was a faint, derisive singsong in the night.

He waited.

144

She waited again. She couldn't bear waiting long, though, and continued:

"I been to the carnival over in Cape City. Tom Carmody drove me. We—we talked to the carny-boss, Charlie, we did, we did, we *sure* did!" And she sort of giggled to herself, secretly.

Charlie was ice-cold. He stirred upright on an elbow.

She said, "We found out what it is in your jar, Charlie——" insinuatingly.

Charlie flumped over, hands to ears. "I don't wanna hear!"

"Oh, but you gotta hear, Charlie. It's a good joke. Oh, it's rare, Charlie," she hissed.

"Go away," he said.

"Unh-unh! No, no, sir, Charlie. Why, no, Charlie—honey. Not until I tell!"

"Git!" he said.

"Let me tell! We talked to that carny-boss, and he—he liked to die laughin'. He said he sold that jar and what was in it to some, some—hick—for twelve bucks. And it ain't worth more'n two bucks at most!"

Laughter bloomed in the dark, right out of her mouth, an awful kind of laughter.

She finished it, quick:

"It's just junk, Charlie! Rubber, papier-mâché, silk, cotton, boric acid! That's all! Got a metal frame inside! That's all it is, Charlie. That's all!" she shrilled.

"No, no!"

He sat up swiftly, ripping sheets apart in big fingers, roaring.

"I don't wanna hear! Don't wanna hear!" he bellowed over and over.

She said, "Wait'll everyone hears how fake it is! Won't they laugh! Won't they flap their lungs!"

He caught her wrists. "You ain't gonna tell them?"

145

"Wouldn't want me known as a liar, would you, Charlie?"

He flung her off and away.

"Whyncha leave me alone? You dirty! Dirty jealous mean of ever'thing I do. I took shine off your nose when I brung the jar home. You didn' sleep right 'til you ruined things!"

She laughed. "Then I won't tell anybody," she said.

He stared at her. "You spoiled *my* fun. That's all that counted. It don't matter if you tell the rest. *I* know. And I'll never have no more fun. You and that Tom Carmody. I wish I could stop him laughin'. He's been laughin' for years at me! Well, you just go tell the rest, the other people, now—might as well have your fun——!"

He strode angrily, grabbed the jar so it sloshed, and would have flung it on the floor, but he stopped trembling, and let it down softly on the spindly table. He leaned over it, sobbing. If he lost this, the world was gone. And he was losing Thedy, too. Every month that passed she danced further away, sneering at him, funning him. For too many years her hips had been the pendulum by which he reckoned the time of his living. But other men—Tom Carmody, for one—were reckoning time from the same source.

Thedy stood waiting for him to smash the jar. Instead, he petted and stroked and gradually quieted himself over it. He thought of the long, good evenings in the past month, those rich evenings of friends and talk, moving about the room. That, at least, was good, if nothing else.

He turned slowly to Thedy. She was lost forever to him.

"Thedy, you didn't go to the carnival."

"Yes, I did."

"You're lyin'," he said quietly.

"No, I'm not!"

"This—this jar *has* to have somethin' in it. Somethin' besides the junk you say. Too many people believe there's somethin' in it, Thedy. You can't change that. The carny-boss, if you talked with him, he lied." Charlie took a deep breath and then said, "Come here, Thedy."

"What you want?" she asked sullenly.

"Come over here."

He took a step toward her. "Come here."

"Keep away from me, Charlie."

"Just want to show you somethin', Thedy." His voice was soft, low, and insistent. "Here, kittie. Here, kittie, kittie, kittie—HERE, KITTIE!"

It was another night, about a week later. Gramps Medknowe and Granny Carnation came, followed by young Juke and Mrs. Tridden and Jahdoo, the colored man. Followed by all the others, young and old, sweet and sour, creaking into chairs, each with his or her thought, hope, fear, and wonder in mind. Each not looking at the shrine, but saying hello softly to Charlie.

They waited for the others to gather. From the shine of their eyes one could see that each saw something different in the jar, something of the life and the pale life after life, and the life in death and the death in life, each with his story, his cue, his lines, familiar, old but new.

Charlie sat alone.

"Hello, Charlie." Somebody peered into the empty bedroom. "Your wife gone off again to visit her folks?"

"Yeah, she run for Tennessee. Be back in a couple weeks. She's the darndest one for runnin'. You know Thedy."

"Great one for jumpin' around, that woman."

Soft voices talking, getting settled, and then, quite suddenly, walking on the dark porch and shining his eyes in at the people—Tom Carmody.

Tom Carmody standing outside the door, knees sagging and trembling, arms hanging and shaking at his side, staring into the room. Tom Carmody not daring to enter. Tom Carmody with his mouth open, but not smiling. His lips wet and slack, not smiling. His face pale as chalk, as if it had been sick for a long time.

Gramps looked up at the jar, cleared his throat and said, "Why, I never noticed so definite before. It's got *blue* eyes."

"It always had blue eyes," said Granny Carnation.

"No," whined Gramps. "No, it didn't. They was brown last time we was here." He blinked upward. "And another thing—it's got brown hair. Didn't have brown hair *before!*"

"Yes, yes, it did," sighed Mrs. Tridden.

"No, it didn't!"

"Yes, it did!"

Tom Carmody, shivering in the summer night, staring in at the jar. Charlie, glancing up at it, rolling a cigarette, casually, all peace and calm, very certain of his life and thoughts. Tom Carmody, alone, seeing things about the jar he never saw before. *Everybody* seeing what they wanted to see; all thoughts running in a fall of quick rain:

"My baby. My little baby," thought Mrs. Tridden.

"A brain!" thought Gramps.

The colored man jigged his fingers. "Middibamboo Mama!"

A fisherman pursed his lips. "Jellyfish!"

"Kitten! Here, kittie, kittie, kittie!" The thoughts drowned clawing in Juke's eyes. "Kitten!"

"Everything and anything!" shrilled Granny's weazened thought. "The night, the swamp, death, the pale things, the wet things from the sea!"

Silence. And then Gramps whispered, "I wonder. Wonder if it's a he—or a she—or just a plain old *it?*"

Charlie glanced up, satisfied, tamping his cigarette, shaping it to his mouth. Then he looked at Tom Carmody, who would never smile again, in the door. "I reckon we'll never know. Yeah, I reckon we won't." Charlie shook his head slowly and settled down with his guests, looking, looking.

It was just one of those things they keep in a jar in the tent of a sideshow on the outskirts of a little, drowsy town. One of those pale things drifting in alcohol plasma, forever dreaming and circling, with its peeled, dead eyes staring out at you and never seeing you. . . .

A Lot on His Mind
by Bill Pronzini

Arbagast was drunk in bed when the police came.

They told the old lady who had let them in to make some coffee, and then they took Arbagast into the bathroom and put him under a cold shower. They kept him there until he started to come out of it, and by that time the coffee was ready. They fed him cup after cup, hot and black, holding him upright on a straight-backed chair.

When they were certain he was sober enough to understand, they told him they had caught the man who had run down and killed his wife four months before.

Arbagast did not say anything for a long while. When he finally spoke, the sound of his voice made one of the policemen shudder involuntarily. "Who was it?"

"A man named Philip Colineaux," the policeman who had shuddered said. "He was involved in another hit-and-run tonight, and this time we got him."

"Someone else was killed?"

"No. He sideswiped a car at an intersection and kept going. There was a patrol car in the vicinity, and they chased him a couple of blocks and flagged him over."

"Was he drinking?"

"Not this time, anyway," the other policeman said. "They took him down for the test, and he passed that all right, but he was pretty shook up. He made a few slips, and that's how we found out about the other time."

"Did he confess to it?"

"Yes," the first policeman said. "He told us he didn't see her. He's a stockbroker and had a lot on his mind. Preoccupied, he called it."

"Speeding?"

"He says no. But he was punching near forty when he hit that car tonight. You can bet he wasn't crawling the other time either."

"Have you got him in jail now?"

The first policeman shook his head, watching Arbagast. There was something about the way he was sitting there, rigid, his eyes flat and unblinking, showing nothing, that made the policeman feel cold. He said, "His lawyer came down and got him out on bail."

"All right," Arbagast said. "Thank you for coming by to tell me."

The two policemen looked at each other, hesitant to leave. The first one said, "Mr. Arbagast, we know you've had a terrible loss. You're taking it pretty hard, and that's understandable. But, well . . ."

He faltered, groping for words. Arbagast looked at him steadily, his face impassive.

"What I'm trying to say, Mr. Arbagast," the policeman went on finally, "the law's going to take care of this one good and proper. We've got him on a manslaughter now, and he had the damage to his car fixed by some friend without reporting it. That's compounding a felony."

"Yes?" Arbagast said.

"So if I were you, I'd just try to forget about the whole thing. It took some time, but we got him, and that's the end of it. Sure, it won't bring your wife back, and it's damned little consolation, but he's going to be punished for what he did. You can rest assured of that."

The policeman paused, trying to read Arbagast's eyes, but they were inscrutable. He seemed about to go on, and then changed his mind. He said only, "I guess that's about it."

"Thank you again for stopping by," Arbagast said.

The two policemen went to the door. "Well, good night," the first one said.

"Yes," Arbagast said. "Good night."

When they had gone, Arbagast lay down on the bed, his hands clasped beneath his head, and stared up at the darkened ceiling. There was a bottle of whiskey on the nightstand, but he did not touch that. He only lay thinking, staring up at the ceiling, until the first gray light of dawn began to filter through the single window.

Arbagast got up then and went to the closet and took the City Telephone Directory from a shelf there. Then he dressed slowly and shaved and went downstairs to his car. He drove across town to the address he had found in the telephone book and parked across the street. He sat there, looking over at the white frame house where Philip Colineaux lived.

It was a nice house, well kept, freshly painted. A flag-stone walk led through a garden alive in color, and there was a high green hedge bordering the right side of the property, near the garage.

Arbagast sat staring across the street. Eight o'clock came, and then nine. No one ventured out. Colineaux wasn't going to work today. Not today.

Arbagast returned to the small furnished room. He made some coffee and fried two eggs, and then he took the gun from the closet and broke it down and oiled and cleaned it. He put shells in the chambers, spinning the cylinder, and, when he was satisfied, put on the safety and slipped it into the pocket of his overcoat.

That night, just after dark, he drove to Philip Colineaux's house and parked across the street, as he had done that morning. He sat there in the darkness until ten o'clock. There were lights in the front room, but the windows were curtained and he could not see inside. No one came out.

The following morning, Arbagast was there again at dawn. He waited until almost noon. There was no sign of activity from inside the house.

At dusk he set up his vigil once more. Shortly past nine, the porch light came on above the door. Arbagast sat up in the seat, his hand touching the gun in his coat pocket.

A man came out onto the porch, standing in the light. There was a woman behind him, in the doorway. *Going out to get some air,* Arbagast thought. *He's been in there two days. But he won't drive.*

The woman shut the door after a moment, and the man stood alone on the porch. He was short, past forty, dressed in slacks and a light windbreaker; hatless. Even at the distance across the street, Arbagast could see that his features were nondescript; it was not the face you would expect to see on a killer.

The man came down the steps and began to walk along the flagstone walk toward the street. Arbagast got out of the car, his fingers clenching on the gun in his pocket, and walked quickly across the deserted street. The man stopped in the shadows of the green hedge as he approached, frowning slightly.

Arbagast said, "Colineaux? Philip Colineaux?"

"Yes?" the man said.

Arbagast stared into his eyes. "My name is Walter Arbagast."

The name did not immediately mean anything to Colineaux. "Yes?" he said again.

153

Arbagast took the gun from his pocket. Colineaux made a half-step backward, his eyes bulging. "My God, what—?"

"Come with me, please," Arbagast said.

"With you?" Colineaux said blankly.

"That's my car across the street."

Colineaux shook his head, not comprehending. "Who are you?" he said. "What is it you want?"

"My name is Walter Arbagast. Surely you remember the name, Colineaux."

"No, I . . ."

"Rosa Arbagast was my wife."

Understanding, complete and instant, flooded Colineaux's eyes. His mouth opened as if to speak, but no words came forth. His face paled. Spittle flecked his lips.

"Yes," Arbagast said. "That's right. The woman you murdered."

"Murdered?" Colineaux said. "No! No, listen, it was an accident! It was dark. She was wearing dark clothes. I was thinking about something else, and I didn't see her. She came out of nowhere. Oh, God, it was an accident!"

"You ran her down," Arbagast said. "You ran her down and then left her to die in the street."

The right side of Colineaux's face began to spasm convulsively. His eyes were great wide holes, black, terrified. "I was frightened!" he moaned. "I panicked! Can't you understand how it was?"

"I understand you murdered my wife," Arbagast said without rancor, without emotion.

"What . . . what are you going to do?"

"I'm going to kill you," Arbagast said simply. "I'm going to run you down with my car. The same way you ran my wife down."

"You're mad! You're insane!"

"Yes," Arbagast said. "Perhaps I am."

Colineaux began to sag. It was as if the bones in his body had suddenly liquefied. His mouth opened and a soundless scream bubbled from his throat.

Arbagast pressed the gun against his stomach. "Don't make a sound," he said. "If you do, I'll kill you right here in front of your house, where you stand."

Colineaux seemed about to crumble. Arbagast took his arm and led him across the street. He opened the rear door to the car. "Get inside and lie flat on the seat. Put your hands behind you."

Colineaux was like a child in his fear. Mutely, he obeyed. Arbagast shut the door and got into the front seat. He took the roll of adhesive tape from the glove compartment and began to tape Colineaux's hands and ankles. When he had finished, he put a strip of tape across his mouth.

"If you rise up in the seat," Arbagast said, "I'll stop the car and shoot you in the back of the head. Do you understand?"

There was a strangled whimper from the man in the back seat. Arbagast nodded. He started the car and drove away.

"We're going out to the Western Avenue Extension," he said aloud, for Colineaux to hear. "There's a side road there, leading up to the reservoir. Nobody uses it much anymore."

The quiet suburban street sang beneath the wheels of the car, and that was the only reply.

"Do you know the stretch just before you reach the reservoir?" Arbagast asked. "It's walled by bluffs on two sides. There's no way you can get off the road there."

The night was deep and black and still.

"I'm going to untie you and let you out there," Arbagast said. "I'm going to give you a chance, Colineaux. You can run for your life. That's more of a chance than you gave Rosa."

The street sang faster, faster . . .

Arbagast turned his head slightly, looking into the rear seat. "Do you hear me, Colineaux? Do you—"

He did not see the woman until very nearly the last split second.

The street had been empty, dark. Then, as if by some strange necromancy, she was there, directly in front of him, a shadowy blur with a grotesque white face that seemed to rush at him, hurtling through the night as he stood still, an empyreal vision captured in the yellow glare of his headlights.

Arbagast swung the wheel in terror, his foot crashing down on the brake, just as that monstrous white face seemed about to strike him head on. The car went into a vicious skid, the quiet, still night exploding into the tortured scream of rubber against pavement. One of the wheels went up over the curb, and the rear end scraped the base of a giant eucalyptus tree that grew there, and then the car settled, and died, on the street. The black night was once again silent.

Arbagast threw open the door, leaning out. The woman stood in the middle of the street behind him, an obscure statue. Then she began to walk, moving unsteadily, coming up the street toward him, and he could see her clearly, see her white face shining in the darkness.

It was Rosa's face.

A strangled cry tore from Arbagast's throat. He slammed the door, his hand twisting the ignition key. The starter whirred, whirred, and then caught, and he fought the lever into gear, his hands trembling violently on the wheel, his heart plunging in his chest. He got the car turned, straightened, and then he was pulling away, and the woman, the apparition, grew smaller and smaller in the rearview mirror until she became a speck that was swallowed, digested, by the night.

Oh, my dear God! Arbagast thought. *Oh, my dear God in Heaven!*

He drove three blocks and turned to the right, pulling in at the curb on a poorly lighted street. He shut off the engine, the headlights.

Turning on the seat, he reached into the back and pulled Colineaux to a sitting position. His trembling hands tore the tape from Colineaux's mouth.

"What happened back there?" Colineaux gasped, his voice mirroring the wet, living fear on his face. "What happened?"

Arbagast was unable to answer. He leaned down and unwound the tape from Colineaux's legs, from his hands. He forced words to come then. "Get out," he said. "Get out now."

Colineaux sat there, immobile. He did not understand. He could not believe.

"Get out," Arbagast said again, and wrenched open the rear door.

Colineaux moved. His body came alive, and he scuttled across the seat, hands clawing, pushing himself outside. He hesitated there for only the barest fraction of a second, looking back at Arbagast, and then he began to run.

Arbagast watched him running off, spindle-legged, down the darkened street. After a long moment, he started the car again and drove away in the opposite direction.

Slowly, carefully, keeping well within the legal speed limit, his eyes fixed on the retreating concrete no longer singing beneath his headlights, he drove directly back to his small furnished room.

He was drunk in bed when the police came.

The Man on the Ground
by Robert E. Howard

Cal Reynolds shifted his tobacco quid to the other side of his mouth as he squinted down the dull blue barrel of his Winchester. His jaws worked methodically, their movement ceasing as he found his bead. He froze into rigid immobility; then his finger hooked on the trigger. The crack of the shot sent the echoes rattling among the hills, and like a louder echo came an answering shot. Reynolds flinched down, flattening his rangy body against the earth, swearing softly. A gray flake jumped from one of the rocks near his head, the ricocheting bullet whining off into space. Reynolds involuntarily shivered. The sound was as deadly as the singing of an unseen rattler.

He raised himself gingerly high enough to peer out between the rocks in front of him. Separated from his refuge by a broad level grown with mesquite-grass and prickly-pear rose a tangle of boulders similar to that behind which he crouched. From among these boulders floated a thin wisp of whitish smoke. Reynolds' keen eyes, trained to sun-scorched distances, detected a small circle of dully gleaming blue steel among the rocks. That ring was the muzzle of a rifle, and Reynolds well knew who lay behind that muzzle.

The feud between Cal Reynolds and Esau Brill had been long, for a Texas feud. Up in the Kentucky mountains family wars may straggle on for generations, but the geographical conditions and human temperament of the Southwest were not conducive to long-drawn-out hostilities. There, feuds were generally concluded with appalling suddenness and finality. The stage was a saloon, the streets of a little cow-town, or the open range. Sniping from the laurel was exchanged for the close-range thundering of six-shooters and sawed-off shotguns which decided matters quickly, one way or the other.

The case of Cal Reynolds and Esau Brill was somewhat out of the ordinary. In the first place, the feud concerned only themselves. Neither friends nor relatives were drawn into it. No one, including the participants, knew just how it started. Cal Reynolds merely knew that he had hated Esau Brill most of his life, and that Brill reciprocated. Once as youths they had clashed with the violence and intensity of rival young catamounts. From that encounter Reynolds carried away a knife scar across the edge of his ribs, and Brill a permanently impaired eye. It had decided nothing. They had fought to a bloody gasping deadlock, and neither had felt any desire to "shake hands and make up." That is a hypocrisy developed in civilization, where men have no stomach for fighting to the death. After a man has felt his adversary's knife grate against his bones, his adversary's thumb gouging at his eyes, his adversary's boot-heels stamped into his mouth, he is scarcely inclined to forgive and forget, regardless of the original merits of the argument.

So Reynolds and Brill carried their mutual hatred into manhood, and as cowpunchers riding for rival ranches, it followed that they found opportunities to carry on their private war. Reynolds rustled cattle from Brill's boss, and Brill returned the compliment. Each raged at the other's tactics, and considered himself justified in eliminating his enemy in any way he could. Brill caught Reynolds without his gun one night in a saloon at Cow Wells, and only an ignominious flight out the back way, with bullets barking at his heels, saved the Reynolds scalp.

Again Reynolds, lying in the chaparral, neatly knocked his enemy out of his saddle at five hundred yards with a .30-30 slug, and, but for the inopportune appearance of a line-rider, the feud would have ended there, Reynolds deciding, in the face of this witness, to forgo his original intention of leaving his covert and hammering out the wounded man's brains with his rifle butt.

Brill recovered from his wound, having the vitality of a longhorn bull, in common with all his sun-leathered iron-thewed breed, and as soon as he was on his feet, he came gunning for the man who had waylaid him.

Now after these onsets and skirmishes, the enemies faced each other at good rifle range, among the lonely hills where interruption was unlikely.

For more than an hour they had lain among the rocks, shooting at each hint of movement. Neither had scored a hit, though the .30-30s whistled perilously close.

In each of Reynolds' temples a tiny pulse hammered maddeningly. The sun beat down on him, and his shirt was soaked with sweat. Gnats swarmed about his head, getting into his eyes, and he cursed venomously. His wet hair was plastered to his scalp; his eyes burned with the glare of the sun, and the rifle barrel was hot to his calloused hand. His right leg was growing numb and he shifted it cautiously, cursing at the jingle of the spur, though he knew Brill could not hear. All this discomfort added fuel to the fire of his wrath. Without process of conscious reasoning, he attributed all his suffering to his enemy. The sun beat dazingly on his sombrero, and his thoughts were slightly addled. It was hotter than the hearthstone of hell among those bare rocks. His dry tongue caressed his baked lips.

Through the muddle of his brain burned his hatred of Esau Brill. It had become more than an emotion: it was an obsession, a monstrous incubus. When he flinched from the whipcrack of Brill's rifle, it was not from fear of death, but because the thought of dying at the hands of his foe was an intolerable horror that made his brain rock with red frenzy. He would have thrown his life away recklessly, if by so doing he could have sent Brill into eternity just three seconds ahead of himself.

He did not analyze these feelings. Men who live by their hands have little time for self-analysis. He was no more aware of the quality of his hate for Esau Brill than he was consciously aware of his hands and feet. It was part of him, and more than part: it enveloped him, engulfed him; his mind and body were no more than its material manifestations. He *was* the hate; it was the whole soul and spirit of him. Unhampered by the stagnant and enervating shackles of sophistication and intellectuality, his instincts rose sheer from the naked primitive. And from them crystallized an almost tangible abstraction—a hate too strong for even death to destroy; a hate powerful enough to embody itself in itself, without the aid or the necessity of material substance.

For perhaps a quarter of an hour neither rifle had spoken. As instinct with death as rattlesnakes coiled among the rocks soaking up poison from the sun's rays, the feudists lay, each waiting his chance, playing the game of endurance until the taut nerves of one or the other should snap.

It was Esau Brill who broke. Not that his collapse took the form of any wild madness or nervous explosion. The wary instincts of the wild were too strong in him for that. But suddenly, with a screamed curse, he hitched up on his elbow and fired blindly at the tangle of stones which concealed his enemy. Only the upper part of his arm and the corner of his blue-shirted shoulder were for an instant visible. That was enough. In that flash-second Cal Reynolds jerked the trigger, and a frightful yell told him his bullet had found its mark. And at the animal pain in that yell, reason and lifelong instincts were swept away by an insane flood of terrible joy. He did not whoop exultantly and spring to his feet, but his teeth bared in a wolfish grin and he involuntarily raised his head. Waking instinct jerked him down again. It was chance that undid him. Even as he ducked back, Brill's answering shot cracked.

Cal Reynolds did not hear it, because, simultaneously with the sound, something exploded in his skull, plunging him into utter blackness, shot briefly with red sparks.

The blackness was only momentary. Cal Reynolds glared wildly around, realizing with a frenzied shock that he was lying in the open. The impact of the shot had sent him rolling from among the rocks, and in that quick instant he realized that it had not been a direct hit. Chance had sent the bullet glancing from a stone, apparently to flick his scalp in passing. That was not so important. What was important was that he was lying out in full view, where Esau Brill could fill him full of lead. A wild glance showed his rifle lying close by. It had fallen across a stone and lay with the stock against the ground, the barrel slanting upward. Another glance showed his enemy standing upright among the stones that had concealed him.

In that one glance Cal Reynolds took in the details of the tall, rangy figure: the stained trousers sagging with the weight of the holstered six-shooter, the legs tucked into the worn leather boots; the streak of crimson on the shoulder of the blue shirt, which was plastered to the wearer's body with sweat; the tousled black hair, from which perspiration was pouring down the unshaven face. He caught the glint of yellow tobacco-stained teeth shining in a savage grin. Smoke still drifted from the rifle in Brill's hands.

These familiar and hated details stood out in startling clarity during the fleeting instant while Reynolds struggled madly against the unseen chains which seemed to hold him to the earth. Even as he thought of the paralysis a glancing blow on the head might induce, something seemed to snap and he rolled free. Rolled is hardly the word: he seemed almost to dart to the rifle that lay across the rock, so light his limbs felt.

Dropping behind the stone, he seized the weapon. He did not even have to lift it. As it lay it bore directly on the man who was now approaching.

His hand was momentarily halted by Esau Brill's strange behavior. Instead of firing or leaping back into cover, the man came straight on, his rifle in the crook of his arm, that damnable leer still on his unshaven lips. Was he mad? Could he not see that his enemy was up again, raging with life, and with a cocked rifle aimed at his heart? Brill seemed not to be looking at him, but to one side, at the spot where Reynolds had just been lying.

Without seeking further for the explanation of his foe's actions, Cal Reynolds pulled the trigger. With the vicious spang of the report a blue shred leaped from Brill's broad breast. He staggered back, his mouth flying open. And the look on his face froze Reynolds again. Esau Brill came of a breed which fights to its last gasp. Nothing was more certain than that he would go down pulling the trigger blindly until the last red vestige of life left him. Yet the ferocious triumph was wiped from his face with the crack of the shot, to be replaced by an awful expression of dazed surprise. He made no move to lift his rifle, which slipped from his grasp, nor did he clutch at his wound. Throwing out his hands in a strange,

stunned, helpless way, he reeled backward on slowly buck-
ling legs, his features frozen into a mask of stupid amazement that made his watcher shiver with its cosmic horror.

Through the opened lips gushed a tide of blood, dyeing
the damp shirt. And like a tree that sways and rushes
suddenly earthward, Esau Brill crashed down on the
mesquite-grass and lay motionless.

Cal Reynolds rose, leaving the rifle where it lay. The
rolling grass-grown hills swam misty and indistinct to his
gaze. Even the sky and the blazing sun had a hazy, unreal
aspect. But a savage content was in his soul. The long feud
was over at last, and whether he had taken his death-wound
or not, he had sent Esau Brill to blaze the trail to hell ahead
of him.

Then he started violently as his gaze wandered to the spot
where he had rolled after being hit. He glared; were his eyes
playing him tricks? Yonder in the grass Esau Brill lay
dead—yet only a few feet away stretched another body.

Rigid with surprise, Reynolds glared at the rangy figure,
slumped grotesquely beside the rocks. It lay partly on its
side, as if flung there by some blind convulsion, the arms
outstretched, the fingers crooked as if blindly clutching. The
short-cropped sandy hair was splashed with blood, and from
a ghastly hole in the temple the brains were oozing. From a
corner of the mouth seeped a thin trickle of tobacco juice to
stain the dusty neck-cloth.

And as he gazed, an awful familiarity made itself evident.
He knew the feel of those shiny leather wrist-bands; he knew
with fearful certainty whose hands had buckled that gunbelt;
the tang of that tobacco juice was still on his palate.

In one brief destroying instant he knew he was looking
down at his own lifeless body. And with the knowledge came
true oblivion.

The Kill
by Peter Fleming

In the cold waiting room of a small railway station in the west
of England two men were sitting. They had sat there for an
hour, and were likely to sit there longer. There was a thick
fog outside. Their train was indefinitely delayed.

The waiting room was a barren and unfriendly place. A
naked electric bulb lit it with wan, disdainful efficiency. A
notice, NO SMOKING, stood on the mantelpiece; when you
turned it around, it said NO SMOKING on the other side, too.
Printed regulations relating to an outbreak of swine fever in
1924 were pinned neatly to one wall, almost, but maddeningly not quite, in the center of it. The stove gave out a hot,
thick smell, powerful already but increasing. A pale leprous
flush on the black and beaded window showed that a light
was burning on the platform outside, in the fog. Somewhere
water dripped with infinite reluctance onto corrugated iron.

The two men sat facing each other over the stove on chairs
of an unswerving woodenness. Their acquaintance was no
older than their vigil. From such talk as they had had, it
seemed likely that they were to remain strangers.

The younger of the two resented the lack of contact in

their relationship more than the lack of comfort in their surroundings. His attitude towards his fellow beings had but recently undergone a transition from the subjective to the objective. As with many of his class and age, the routine, unrecognized as such, of an expensive education, with the triennial alternative of those delights normal to wealth and gentility, had atrophied many of his curiosities. For the first twenty-odd years of his life he had read humanity in terms of relevance rather than reality, looking on people who held no ordained place in his own existence much as a buck in a park watches visitors walking up the drive: mildly, rather resentfully inquiring—not inquisitive. Now, hot in reaction from this unconscious provincialism, he treated mankind as a museum, gaping conscientiously at each fresh exhibit, hunting for the noncumulative evidence of man's complexity with indiscriminate zeal. To each magic circle of individuality he saw himself as a kind of free-lance tangent. He aspired to be a connoisseur of men.

There was undoubtedly something arresting about the specimen before him. Of less than medium height, the stranger had yet that sort of ranging leanness that lends vicarious inches. He wore a long black overcoat, very shabby, and his shoes were covered with mud. His face had no color in it, though the impression it produced was not one of pallor; the skin was of a dark sallow, tinged with gray. The nose was pointed, the jaw sharp and narrow. Deep vertical wrinkles, running down towards it from the high cheekbones, sketched the permanent groundwork of a broader smile than the deep-set honey-colored eyes seemed likely to authorize. The most striking thing about the face was the incongruity of its frame. On the back of his head the stranger wore a bowler hat with a very narrow brim. No word of such casual implications as a tilt did justice to its angle. It was clamped, by something at least as holy as custom, to the back of his skull, and that thin, questing face confronted the world fiercely from under a black halo of nonchalance. The man's whole appearance suggested *difference* rather than aloofness. The unnatural way he wore his hat had the significance of indirect comment, like the antics of a performing animal. It was as if he were part of some older thing, of which *Homo sapiens* in a bowler hat was an expurgated edition. He sat with his shoulders hunched and his hands thrust into his overcoat pockets. The hint of discomfort in his attitude seemed due not so much to the fact that his chair was hard as to the fact that it was a chair.

The young man had found him uncommunicative. The most mobile sympathy, launching consecutive attacks on different fronts, had failed to draw him out. The reserved adequacy of his replies conveyed a rebuff more effectively than sheer surliness. Except to answer him, he did not look at the young man. When he did, his eyes were full of an abstracted amusement. Sometimes he smiled, but for no immediate cause.

Looking back down their hour together, the young man saw a field of endeavor on which frustrated banalities lay thick, like the discards of a routed army. But resolution, curiosity, and the need to kill time all clamored against an admission of defeat.

"If he will not talk," thought the young man, "then I will. The sound of my own voice is infinitely preferable to the sound of none. I will tell him what has just happened to me. It is really a most extraordinary story. I will tell it as well as I can, and I shall be very much surprised if its impact on his mind does not shock this man into some form of self-revelation. He is unaccountable without being *outré,* and I am inordinately curious about him."

Aloud he said, in a brisk and engaging manner: "I think you said you were a hunting man?"

The other raised his quick, honey-colored eyes. They gleamed with inaccessible amusement. Without answering, he lowered them again to contemplate the little beads of light thrown through the ironwork of the stove onto the skirts of his overcoat. Then he spoke. He had a husky voice.

"I came here to hunt," he agreed.

"In that case," said the young man, "you will have heard of Lord Fleer's private pack. Their kennels are not far from here."

"I know them," replied the other.

"I have just been staying there," the young man continued. "Lord Fleer is my uncle."

The other looked up, smiled, and nodded, with the bland inconsequence of a foreigner who does not understand what is being said to him. The young man swallowed his impatience.

"Would you," he continued, using a slightly more peremptory tone than heretofore, "would you care to hear a new and rather remarkable story about my uncle? Its dénouement is not two days old. It is quite short."

From the vastness of some hidden joke, those light eyes mocked the necessity of a definite answer. At length: "Yes," said the stranger, "I would." The impersonality in his voice might have passed for a parade of sophistication, a reluctance to betray interest. But the eyes hinted that interest was alive elsewhere.

"Very well," said the young man.

Drawing his chair a little closer to the stove, he began:

As perhaps you know, my uncle, Lord Fleer, leads a retired though by no means an inactive life. For the last two or three hundred years, the currents of contemporary thought have passed mainly through the hands of men whose gregarious instincts have been constantly awakened and almost invariably indulged. By the standards of the

168

eighteenth century, when Englishmen first became self-conscious about solitude, my uncle would have been considered unsociable. In the early nineteenth century, those not personally acquainted with him would have thought him romantic. Today, his attitude towards the sound and fury of modern life is too negative to excite comment as an oddity; yet even now, were he to be involved in any occurrence which could be called disastrous or interpreted as discreditable, the press would pillory him as a "Titled Recluse."

The truth of the matter is, my uncle has discovered the elixir, or, if you prefer it, the opiate, of self-sufficiency. A man of extremely simple tastes, not cursed with overmuch imagination, he sees no reason to cross frontiers of habit which the years have hallowed into rigidity. He lives in his castle (it may be described as commodious rather than comfortable), runs his estate at a slight profit, shoots a little, rides a great deal, and hunts as often as he can. He never sees his neighbors except by accident, thereby leading them to suppose, with sublime but unconscious arrogance, that he must be slightly mad. If he is, he can at least claim to have padded his own cell.

My uncle has never married. As the only son of his only brother, I was brought up in the expectation of being his heir. During the war, however, an unforeseen development occurred.

In this national crisis my uncle, who was of course too old for active service, showed a lack of public spirit which earned him locally a good deal of unpopularity. Briefly, he declined to recognize the war, or, if he did recognize it, gave no sign of having done so. He continued to lead his own vigorous but (in the circumstances) rather irrelevant life. Though he found himself at last obliged to recruit his hunt servants from men of advanced age and uncertain mettle in any crisis of the chase, he contrived to mount them well, and twice a week during the season himself rode two horses to a standstill after the hill foxes which, as no doubt you know, provide the best sport the Fleer country has to offer.

When the local gentry came and made representations to him, saying that it was time he did something for his country besides destroying its vermin by the most unreliable and expensive method ever devised, my uncle was very sensible. He now saw, he said, that he had been standing too aloof from a struggle of whose progress (since he never read the paper) he had been only indirectly aware. The next day he wrote to London and ordered *The Times* and a Belgian refugee. It was the least he could do, he said. I think he was right.

The Belgian refugee turned out to be a female, and dumb. Whether one or both of these characteristics had been stipulated for by my uncle, nobody knew. At any rate, she took up her quarters at Fleer: a heavy, unattractive girl of twenty-five, with a shiny face and short black hairs on the backs of her hands. Her life appeared to be modeled on that of the larger ruminants, except, of course, that the greater part of it took place indoors. She ate a great deal, slept with a will, and had a bath every Sunday, remitting this salubrious custom only when the housekeeper, who enforced it, was away on her holiday. Much of her time she spent sitting on a sofa, on the landing outside her bedroom, with Prescott's *Conquest of Mexico* open on her lap. She read either exceptionally slowly or not at all, for to my knowledge she carried the first volume about with her for eleven years. Hers, I think, was the contemplative type of mind.

The curious, and from my point of view the unfortunate, aspect of my uncle's patriotic gesture was the gradually increasing affection with which he came to regard this unlovable creature. Although, or more probably because, he saw her only at meals, when her features were rather more animated than at other times, his attitude towards her passed from the detached to the courteous, and from the courteous to the paternal. At the end of the war there was no question of her return to Belgium, and one day in 1919 I heard with pardonable mortification that my uncle had legally adopted her, and was altering his will in her favor.

Time, however, reconciled me to being disinherited by a being who, between meals, could scarcely be described as sentient. I continued to pay an annual visit to Fleer, and to ride with my uncle after his big-boned Welsh hounds over the sullen, dark gray hill country in which—since its possession was no longer assured to me—I now began to see a powerful, though elusive, beauty.

I came down here three days ago, intending to stay for a week. I found my uncle, who is a tall, fine-looking man with a beard, in his usual unassailable good health. The Belgian, as always, gave me the impression of being impervious to disease, to emotion, or indeed to anything short of an act of God. She had been putting on weight since she came to live with my uncle, and was now a very considerable figure of a woman, though not, as yet, unwieldly.

It was at dinner, on the evening of my arrival, that I first noticed a certain *malaise* behind my uncle's brusque, laconic manner. There was evidently something on his mind. After dinner he asked me to come into his study. I detected, in the delivery of the invitation, the first hint of embarrassment I had known him to betray.

The walls of the study were hung with maps and the extremities of foxes. The room was littered with bills, catalogues, old gloves, fossils, rat-traps, cartridges, and feathers which had been used to clean his pipe—a stale diversity of jetsam which somehow managed to produce an impression of relevance and continuity, like the debris in an animal's lair. I had never been in the study before.

"Paul," said my uncle as soon as I had shut the door, "I am very much disturbed."

I assumed an air of sympathetic inquiry.

"Yesterday," my uncle went on, "one of my tenants came to see me. He is a decent man who farms a strip of land outside the park wall to the northward. He said that he had lost two sheep in a manner for which he was wholly unable to account. He said he thought they had been killed by some wild animal."

My uncle paused. The gravity of his manner was really portentous.

"Dogs?" I suggested, with the slightly patronizing diffidence of one who has probability on his side.

My uncle shook his head judiciously. "This man had often seen sheep which had been killed by dogs. He said that they were always badly torn—nipped about the legs, driven into a corner, worried to death; it was never a clean piece of work. These two sheep had not been killed like that. I went down to see them for myself. Their throats had been torn out. They were not bitten or nuzzled. They had both died in the open, not in a corner. Whatever did it was an animal more powerful and more cunning than a dog."

I said, "It couldn't have been something that had escaped from a traveling menagerie, I suppose?"

"They don't come into this part of the country," replied my uncle; "there are no fairs."

We were both silent for a moment. It was hard not to show more curiosity than sympathy as I waited on some further revelation to stake out my uncle's claim on the latter emotion. I could put no interpretation on those two dead sheep wild enough to account for his evident distress.

He spoke again, but with obvious reluctance.

"Another was killed early this morning," he said in a low voice, "on the Home Farm. In the same way."

For lack of any better comment, I suggested beating the nearby coverts. There might be some——

"We've scoured the woods," interrupted my uncle brusquely.

"And found nothing?"

"Nothing . . . except some tracks."

"What sort of tracks?"

My uncle's eyes were suddenly evasive. He turned his head away.

"They were a man's tracks," he said slowly. A log fell over in the fireplace.

Again a silence. The interview appeared to be causing him pain rather than relief. I decided that the situation could lose nothing through the frank expression of my curiosity. Plucking up courage, I asked him roundly what cause he had to be upset? Three sheep, the property of his tenants, had died deaths which, though certainly unusual, were unlikely to remain for long mysterious. Their destroyer, whatever it was, would inevitably be caught, killed, or driven away in the course of the next few days. The loss of another sheep or two was the worst he had to fear.

When I had finished, my uncle gave me an anxious, almost a guilty look. I was suddenly aware that he had a confession to make.

"Sit down," he said. "I wish to tell you something."

This is what he told me:

A quarter of a century ago, my uncle had had occasion to engage a new housekeeper. With the blend of fatalism and sloth which is the foundation of the bachelor's attitude to the servant problem, he took on the first applicant. She was a tall, black, slant-eyed woman from the Welsh border, aged about thirty. My uncle said nothing about her character, but described her as having "powers." When she had been at Fleer some months, my uncle began to notice her, instead of taking her for granted. She was not averse to being noticed.

One day she came and told my uncle that she was with child by him. He took it calmly enough till he found that she expected him to marry her, or pretended to expect it. Then he flew into a rage, called her a whore, and told her she must leave the house as soon as the child was born. Instead of breaking down or continuing the scene, she began to croon to herself in Welsh, looking at him sideways with a certain amusement. This frightened him. He forbade her to come near him again, had her things moved into an unused wing of the castle, and engaged another housekeeper.

A child was born, and they came and told my uncle that the woman was going to die; she asked for him continually, they said. As much frightened as distressed, he went through passages long unfamiliar to her room. When the woman saw him, she began to gabble in a preoccupied kind of way, looking at him all the time, as if she were repeating a lesson. Then she stopped, and asked that he be shown the child.

It was a boy. The midwife, my uncle noticed, handled it with a reluctance almost amounting to disgust.

"That is your heir," said the dying woman in a harsh, unstable voice. "I have told him what he is to do. He will be a good son to me, and jealous of his birthright." And she went off, my uncle said, into a wild yet cogent rigmarole about a curse, embodied in the child, which would fall on any whom he made his heir over the bastard's head. At last her voice trailed away, and she fell back, exhausted and staring.

As my uncle turned to go, the midwife whispered to him to look at the child's hands. Gently unclasping the podgy, futile little fists, she showed him that on each hand the third finger was longer than the second. . . .

Here I interrupted. The story had a certain queer force behind it, perhaps from its obvious effect on the teller. My uncle feared and hated the things he was saying.

"What did that mean," I asked, "—the third finger longer than the second?"

"It took me a long time to discover," replied my uncle.

"My own servants, when they saw that I did not know, would not tell me. But at last I found out through the doctor, who had it from an old woman in the village. People born with their third finger longer than their second become werewolves. At least"—he made a perfunctory effort at amused indulgence—"that is what the common people here think."

"And what does that—what is that supposed to mean?" I too found myself throwing rather hasty sops to skepticism. I was growing strangely credulous.

"A werewolf," said my uncle, dabbling in improbability without self-consciousness, "is a human being who becomes, at intervals, to all intents and purposes a wolf. The transformation—or the supposed transformation—takes place at night. The werewolf kills men and animals, and is supposed to drink their blood. Its preference is for men. All through the Middle Ages, down to the seventeenth century, there were innumerable cases (especially in France) of men and women being legally tried for offenses which they had committed as animals. Like the witches, they were rarely acquitted, but, unlike the witches, they seem seldom to have been unjustly condemned." My uncle paused. "I have been reading the old books," he explained. "I wrote to a man in London who is interested in these things when I heard what was believed about the child."

"What became of the child?" I asked.

"The wife of one of my keepers took it in," said my uncle. "She was a stolid woman from the North who, I think, welcomed the opportunity to show what little store she set by the local superstitions. The boy lived with them till he was ten. Then he ran away. I had not heard of him since then till"—my uncle glanced at me almost apologetically—"till yesterday."

We sat for a moment in silence, looking at the fire. My

imagination had betrayed my reason in its full surrender to the story. I had not got it in me to dispel his fears with a parade of sanity. I was a little frightened myself.

"You think it is your son, the werewolf, who is killing the sheep?" I said at length.

"Yes. For a boast, or for a warning, or perhaps out of spite, at a night's hunting wasted."

"Wasted?"

My uncle looked at me with troubled eyes.

"His business is not with sheep," he said uneasily.

For the first time I realized the implications of the Welsh-woman's curse. The hunt was up. The quarry was the heir to Fleer. I was glad to have been disinherited.

"I have told Germaine not to go out after dusk," said my uncle, coming in pat on my train of thought.

The Belgian was called Germaine; her other name was Vom.

I confess I spent no very tranquil night. My uncle's story had not wholly worked in me that "suspension of disbelief" which someone speaks of as being the prime requisite of good drama. But I have a powerful imagination. Neither fatigue nor common sense could quite banish the vision of that metamorphosed malignancy ranging, with design, the black and silver silences outside my window. I found myself listening for the sound of loping footfalls on a frost-baked crust of beech leaves. . . .

Whether it was in my dream that I heard, once, the sound of howling, I do not know. But the next morning I saw, as I dressed, a man walking quickly up the drive. He looked like a shepherd. There was a dog at his heels, trotting with a noticeable lack of assurance. At breakfast my uncle told me that another sheep had been killed, almost under the noses of the watchers. His voice shook a little. Solicitude sat oddly on his features as he looked at Germaine. She was eating porridge, as if for a wager.

After breakfast we decided on a campaign. I will not weary you with the details of its launching and its failure. All day we quartered the woods with thirty men, mounted and on foot. Near the scene of the kill our dogs picked up a scent which they followed for two miles and more, only to lose it on the railway line. But the ground was too hard for tracks, and the men said it could only have been a fox or a polecat, so surely and readily did the dogs follow it.

The exercise and the occupation were good for our nerves. But late in the afternoon my uncle grew anxious; twilight was closing in swiftly under a sky heavy with clouds, and we were some distance from Fleer. He gave final instructions for the penning of the sheep by night, and we turned our horses' heads for home.

We approached the castle by the back drive, which was little used: a dank, unholy alley, running the gauntlet of a belt of firs and laurels. Beneath our horses' hooves flints chinked remotely under a thick carpet of moss. Each consecutive cloud from their nostrils hung with an air of permanency, as if bequeathed to the unmoving air.

We were perhaps three hundred yards from the tall gates leading to the stableyard when both horses stopped dead, simultaneously. Their heads were turned towards the trees on our right, beyond which, I knew, the sweep of the main drive converged on ours.

My uncle gave a short, inarticulate cry in which premonition stood aghast at the foreseen. At the same moment something howled on the other side of the trees. There was relish, and a kind of sobbing laughter, in that hateful sound. It rose and fell luxuriously, and rose and fell again, fouling the night. Then it died away, fawning on society in a throaty whimper.

The forces of silence fell unavailingly on its rear; its filthy echoes still went reeling through our heads. We were aware that feet went loping lightly down the iron-hard drive . . . two feet.

My uncle flung himself off his horse and dashed through the trees. I followed. We scrambled down a bank and out into the open. The only figure in sight was motionless.

Germaine Vom lay doubled up in the drive, a solid, black mark against the shifting values of the dusk. We ran forward. . . .

To me she had always been an improbable cipher rather than a real person. I could not help reflecting that she died, as she had lived, in the livestock tradition. Her throat had been torn out.

The young man leant back in his chair, a little dizzy from talking and from the heat of the stove. The inconvenient realities of the waiting room, forgotten in his narrative, closed in on him again. He sighed, and smiled rather apologetically at the stranger.

"It is a wild and improbable story," he said. "I do not expect you to believe the whole of it. For me, perhaps, the reality of its implications has obscured its almost ludicrous lack of verisimilitude. You see, by the death of the Belgian I am heir to Fleer."

The stranger smiled: a slow but no longer an abstracted smile. His honey-colored eyes were bright. Under his long black overcoat his body seemed to be stretching itself in sensual anticipation. He rose silently to his feet.

The other found a sharp, cold fear drilling into his vitals. Something behind those shining eyes threatened him with appalling immediacy, like a sword at his heart. He was sweating. He dared not move.

The stranger's smile was now a grin, a ravening convulsion of the face. His eyes blazed with a hard and purposeful delight. A thread of saliva dangled from the corner of his mouth.

Very slowly he lifted one hand and removed his bowler hat. Of the fingers crooked about its brim, the young man saw that the third was longer than the second.

Serenade for Baboons
by Noel Langley

The Doctor was a chubby, benign little man who had taken his degree in Edinburgh, married, become old-fashioned, and come to South Africa because he had been told that the practices were not overcrowded as they were in Glasgow, and patients were less inclined to demand new-fangled gadgets and fancy remedies for ordinary ailments.

"I am a practical, down-to-earth doctor," he chose to say, "and I don't believe in anything that isn't practical and down-to-earth. A stomach-ache is a stomach-ache, and the gripes is the gripes: and imagination is the enemy of man."

He said this to a fellow-traveller on the Union Castle boat, on his way to Cape Town, and the fellow-traveller had answered: "Then I hope you're wise in going to South Africa."

"I hope so!" the Doctor, who had spent his last capital on his tickets, said with feeling. "I was told there was plenty of room for a competent man!"

"That I wouldn't deny," agreed the fellow-traveller. "It's the imagination that may give you trouble. The rural folks are superstitious, you know."

"I'm sure I can cure them of *that!*" said the Doctor in mild relief. "May it be the least of my problems!"

It proved to be the greatest, however; for when he eventually bought a country practice in a village of tin shanties at the foot of the Drakensberg Mountains, he found his patients hard to woo. They were rugged and taciturn and still resentful of an English accent. When they came to him with the stomach-ache, expecting to have it called a romantic ailment and to be made much of, his airy pooh-pooh and his casual prescriptions of sodium bicarbonate, instead of reassuring them, sent them away discontented.

One day the Doctor learned that an ancient Hottentot witch-doctor called M'Pini was doing better business with the local farmers than he was, and it struck his professional pride in a vulnerable spot. He tried to register a complaint with the Mounted Police when they made their rounds of the district, and he tried to enlist the moral support of Mr. Coetze, the local minister; but in both cases he met with polite evasion. He complained indignantly to his wife, a discreet and reserved Scotch woman who kept her place. "They believe in witchcraft!" he said. "That shrivelled little savage gives them the entrails of animals and burns feathers! I shall fight this out, Agnes, on principle rather than as competition!"

"I was talking with Mrs. Naude," said his wife, referring to the wife of the storekeeper. "She said you'd do well to tolerate the local feeling a wee bitty more than you do. It'd be quicker, she was saying, for you to come round to their way of thinking than to wait for them to come round to yours."

"I would sooner," decreed the Doctor from the bottom of his heart, "become a savage myself."

But it did not help to pay his bills, and when their income was almost gone, she spoke to him again about it.

"A little deception," said the good woman, "need hurt

nobody's conscience when it's in the cause of good. Just a little mumbo-jumbo with their cough medicine is all they want, and pretty names on the labels; and you'd put that Hottentot out of business; and come now, Jamie, how could it hurt you?"

"I'll make no concessions to superstitious folk who should know better," he said doggedly. "They'll come round to my way of thinking, or we'll stay as we are."

"I'm having to borrow from the storekeeper," his wife pointed out.

"I cured him of the toothache," said her husband, "long before the witch-doctor rubbed hippopotamus fat on his silly head; we owe him nothing."

"I'd like to convince him," said his wife sadly.

By now the hostility between the Doctor and the witch-doctor M'Pini was openly recognized. If they passed each other on the dirt roads, it was all the Doctor could do to control himself, but he knew there was nothing to gain by antagonizing the locals further, so he held his peace; though by now he believed fanatically that he stood for the principles of enlightenment and was prepared to die for them.

That he would have is certain, for he still had to eat; but in his hour of need, Fate sent him a client who hated witch-doctors as much as he did. He was a farmer from the wilds of the mountains, called Hoareb, and despite his unprepossessing shape, the Doctor could have wept with joy when he came to his house to have a wound in his arm dressed, and paid his money, and went away again without more than ten words being exchanged between them.

"There goes a patient after my own heart," said the Doctor, even though there wasn't a man in the village who didn't hate the sight of Hoareb and give him a wide berth when they saw him coming, slouching along with his huge shoulders stooped forward, his cold beady eyes sunk so far back into his head that his eyebrows seemed to hang over black pits, and his tight-shut mouth that looked like a badly healed scar across his face. He never stayed longer in the village than necessity kept him, and never came in from his farm up in the mountains more often than he could help.

Some of them put his age at sixty, others at forty, and one or two insisted that he had been up on his farm in the mountains since the Lord put the mountains there, and there he would always be, with his slouching shoulders and snake's eyes, until the Lord sent the mountains to dust on Judgment Day, and plunged Hoareb into everlasting fire.

The Doctor, however, thought of him with pride and satisfaction. He had had to make no concessions to him, and he had gone away satisfied with the Doctor's work. He was the model patient, and the exoneration of the Doctor's rigid principles.

A few days later, as if in substantiation of this, Hoareb came back. He rode unhurriedly through the village, reined his horse up in front of the Doctor's cottage, and banged at the door until he broke the brass knocker the Doctor's wife had brought all the way from Edinburgh. The Doctor was in his bath, but climbed out, sopping wet, and hurried down in his towel to save the door from bursting off its hinges, while his wife hid herself in the kitchen. He unlatched the door, and Hoareb nearly threw him on his back by thrusting his way into the hall without awaiting invitation. "My friend is ill," he said without preamble. "I think perhaps dying. You had better come. Now."

"As soon as I can," the Doctor assured him.

"Now," repeated Hoareb.

"I'll have to dress," the Doctor pointed out. "I'll be ready in ten minutes." He left Hoareb in the hall and scuttled back upstairs to dress, delighted beyond words, and stiff with pride and assurance. He was into his clothes and had his bag packed, back into the hall, in just under ten minutes. Hoareb was standing where he had left him, staring into nothing.

"My horse. Won't take me a minute," said the Doctor, and ran round to the stable. He had two horses so that one was always saddled in readiness. He strapped his bag to the saddle and cantered back to the high street.

Hoareb was mounted, waiting.

As soon as the Doctor appeared, he swung his horse round and set off on the forty-seven miles without a word, and the Doctor fell behind obediently. The village watched them go, and speculation ran high.

The whole of the journey was conducted in silence. After twenty miles the Doctor's elation abated a little, for as they left the flat veld and began climbing the pass up into the Drakensberg, a strong sense of loneliness came over him, and Hoareb's back seemed to grow larger and more ominous. A hundred and one stories of Hoareb's rages, his insane attacks on his natives, his utter secrecy in all he did, came flooding back, though he cast them sternly from his mind, concentrating on the duties of his profession, and thought of the friend—"perhaps dying," Hoareb had said.

They entered the bush growing round the foothills, and when the sunlight was shut out by the squat trees, his nerves began to show the first signs of strain. The path was steep and slippery with moss. Loose pebbles broke away under the horses' feet and made them stumble. Branches whipped him across the face and flicked his ears painfully. Occasionally animals, frightened by their noise, rustled away under the bushes with a suddenness that brought his heart into his mouth, but Hoareb continued on his way stolidly, never once turning in his saddle to see whether the Doctor was still following.

Africa at her wildest lay round them. They passed a small

waterfall and a pool where evil little arrow-heads cut the
water, and larger snakes lay curled beside its edge. Farther
on they came to a headless water-buck at the side of the
path, and here Hoareb reined up and pointed to it with a
twisted finger.

"Baboons done it," he said, and his face twisted with
anger. "Baboons." It came through his teeth with vitriolic
intensity. "Baboons done it. Cursed of God!" His eyes were
pin-points of fanatical hatred. "I tear their heads off, like
they done that, you hear? Like they tear that head off, I tear
theirs! Cursed of God! Cursed of God!" His gaze met the
Doctor's, and the Doctor looked away, discomfited. "You
think I'm afraid of them, maybe? Me, afraid of baboons, the
spawn of Satan? They think I'm afraid of them, too, but every
one I shall kill, by tearing off the head, like that buck, you
hear? I not afraid!" He suddenly stood up in his stirrups and
shouted at the top of his terrific voice: "Do you hear? Cursed
of God! I not afraid! I not afraid! Do you hear?"

The echoes came thundering back from all round them,
and when they had died away he waited for a few seconds,
straining for something he didn't want to hear.

The Doctor held his breath, and felt that the whole of the
wildness about them hung in silent suspense, waiting with
them. The seconds trickled by, and then Hoareb suddenly
threw his head back and bellowed with laughter, a hoarse
laughter more removed from humour than anything the Doctor had ever heard. His horse shied sideways with fear and
he held it to the path with difficulty. Hoareb laughed again,
stopped suddenly, spat at the dead water-buck, and brought
his heels down into his horse's ribs with a vicious kick, then
continued along the path, sinking back into morose silence,
and gazing in front of him.

Another hour's riding through the gloom of the bush
brought them into a clearing where the outbuildings of the

185

farm stood. They were ordinary wattle and tin sheds, daubed with mud and well kept, reassuringly conventional in layout, and yet looking slyly wrong in every line and corner. A few hens were scratching at the rubbish-heap, and from somewhere came the sound of a dog howling, but there was no sign of a human being anywhere in sight.

They rode past the sheds and, turning a clump of wild mimosa, came upon the farmhouse, still and deserted. The howling of the dog grew clearer; it rose mournfully in the stillness, wavered, and sank into a low whine, and then rose again more insistently than before.

Hoareb brought his horse up to the steps of the verandah, let the reins drag, and waited, without speaking, a leather whip thumping against his leg, for the Doctor to dismount. The Doctor swung off his horse, undid his bag and came up to the steps. Hoareb jerked his head over his shoulder.

"Hear dog?" he said. "Maybe you come too late."

"Where is she?" the Doctor asked.

Hoareb turned and went into the house, and he followed unhappily. There was a dank stuffy smell of animals in the dark room, but not of animals the Doctor knew or recognized. As his eyes grew used to the gloom, he found himself in a poorly furnished dining-room with the remains of a meal still on the table. One of the chairs had been broken, and the pieces lay scattered across the floor. In a corner something moved, and he turned with defensive speed to face it. Two children were crouching against the wall, their eyes wide with fear, and as he looked at them, a strange feeling of uncertainty crept over him. There was something more than imbecility in the eyes gazing into his. His mind flew back to animals again, and he remembered a sick gibbon monkey he had once tried to save from dying. It had cried like a human being. The children were about twelve or fourteen, a boy and a girl, dark skinned. He made a movement toward them, and they shrank farther back against the wall. An almost inaudible whimper of terror came from the girl, and he drew back in distress. Hoareb from the other end of the room broke the silence.

"Baboons!" he said. "A fine couple, do you hear?" He came across and stood towering over them, then uncurled the whip and flicked it lightly. The girl began a poor sickly scream that quavered into nothing, and he laughed. "Baboons; do you hear? Look how they fear me! I have only to raise my foot and they squeal. Do you see how they fear me? And you think I am afraid of baboons!" He laughed again, and the whip cracked. "Out! Out of here! Cursed of God!" he shouted with sudden rage. "Back to your filth!"

The two children fled, stumbling in their panic, and he followed them to the door. The boy missed his footing and fell to the ground, cutting his head on the stones. The girl paused, gasping with fright, and helped him scramble to his feet with the blood pouring from his face, and together they disappeared behind the mimosa trees.

The dog, which had been silent for a while, raised its voice again in a long-drawn howl that brought the hair up on the Doctor's neck. Hoareb shouted thickly, and it stopped. He coiled the whip and came back into the room.

"There," he said, and opened a door that had been hidden by a curtain of sacking. "Had an accident. I think perhaps she will die."

The Doctor entered first, and stood stock still for a moment. On a bed by the window lay a middle-aged Zulu woman covered by a blanket. He crossed the room swiftly and bent over her. Her lower jaw had been crushed, and hung at an ugly angle. The blanket was soaked in blood. He moved it slightly and uncovered a gash across her shoulder. He turned his head and saw Hoareb still standing in the door, watching expressionlessly.

"What do you expect me to do?" the Doctor asked with an effort. "This woman's dying."

Hoareb nodded. "Accident," he said.

The Doctor remembered the broken chair. "It's a case for the police and the coroner," he said, "not a doctor."

Hoareb moved slowly across to the bed.

"The police not come here," he said heavily. "If she dies, I bury her."

"You can't do that," the Doctor said briskly, though it took courage; then he heard a faint scratching behind him and turned.

There was a fourth person in the room.

He sat squatting over in a corner; a little wizened, dark shape, older than time, watching them intently.

The Doctor started back, instinctively afraid.

"Who's that?" he asked nervously.

Hoareb followed his glance, and when he saw the little man, he went suddenly mad. He swung his whip in the air with a roar and lunged forward. The Doctor managed to catch his arm in time, and while the whip was still quivering in mid-air, the corner was suddenly empty.

Hoareb stood breathing unevenly, stooped forward and trembling, and then blundered wildly about the room, slashing out at the shadows.

The Doctor had drawn back, for in that moment he had recognized the little witch-doctor, M'Pini, and his rage was as ungovernable as Hoareb's, shuddering through him and making him weak.

The woman on the bed opened her eyes and lay watching them dispassionately, the glaze of death upon her. Hoareb suddenly paused in his crazy search and turned on her wildly.

"You brought him here!" he said thickly. "You brought witch-doctors into my house!"

The whip fell across her body, and the Doctor's mind cleared itself of its momentary fury. He caught Hoareb's arm before the whip fell again, and wrenched the whip out of his hand.

"Are you mad?" he shouted breathlessly. "Get out of here and leave her to die in peace!"

For a moment he thought Hoareb was going to fall upon him barehanded; but instead, he backed slowly to the door, his eyes shrunk to insane pin-points.

"She brought witch-doctors into my house," he mumbled dully. "Cursed of God!" He leant against the doorpost struggling with his breath. "Because I beat her, she brought witch-doctors to kill me!"

"Get out of here!" said the Doctor steadily, realizing that the man was insane with fright and not anger, and handed him back the whip.

Hoareb stood a second, undecided; then with a heavy shambling gait he disappeared through the door, and the Doctor heard him cross the dining-room and go down the steps of the verandah, swearing incoherently.

The woman on the bed stirred, and he came back to her. She was looking up at him and trying to speak. He shook his head gently, but the torn muscles about her jaw still quivered, and he bent closer.

"They come. They come," she whispered, and pointed weakly toward the window. "Look!"

He raised his head and, hearing nothing, slowly moved to the window; and then he stood frozen, unable to take in what he saw outside. The dark had fallen, but he could see, in the centre of the clearing, the motionless figure of Hoareb, his eyes straining out of his head and bright with horror.

Round him in a still, shadowy half-circle, between him and the undergrowth, sat fifty or sixty baboons, sitting as the little man had sat, watching him intently.

No one—nothing—moved.

How long the Doctor stood watching, he did not know. It seemed endless waiting, while outside nothing moved or made a sound. They could all have been stuffed figures in a ghoulish charade: Hoareb standing there staring; the baboons in their half-circle watching him. Even the air was still; even the earth about them seemed to be locked in a moment of time.

A trickle of foam ran down Hoareb's chin. He raised his hand automatically and wiped it away. Then he began to look around him, slowly, as if he were counting them.

But he never moved, and the baboons sat watching him as if they were carved from stone.

The Doctor could hear his own watch ticking like a muffled sledge-hammer in his waistcoat pocket.

Then the chant began—a thin, shining trail of sound that came from nowhere and everywhere; too faint to catch, too loud to shut out of the brain; with no rhythm or beat, no tune, no words. It was the noise of the innocent crying for revenge against the wicked, and Hoareb knew it for that, for he made a blind, groping step toward the house. He had not moved a foot when, as if by magic, the half-circle completed itself.

The baboons came from nowhere.

One moment there was a clear track back to the house; the next, he was surrounded by them, and stood with his body sagging, glaring at them. They sat squatting in the dust, watching him intently; and still the chant went on, without pause, like the drone of flies against a window, or water through dry reeds.

He was shuddering now, and his breath was beginning to come in jerky sobs that shook his body. For a second his frantic gaze met the Doctor's, and the Doctor's spine crawled; but he stood where he was, unable to help.

Then the chant changed, subtly and inexplicably, and

with one liquid movement the baboons closed in until they were half as near again.

Hoareb began to gibber, but still he stood, transfixed, while the circle of baboons sat motionless, watching him still, and the chant continued on and on monotonously. Then he began to laugh.

He began to laugh, low at first, a queer broken chuckle; then it grew to a discordant clatter of hysteria, rolling and echoing back in distorted keys.

The Doctor stood watching, paralysed, until a noise from the bed made him turn his head. The woman had raised her arm above her head. As she did so, the chant gathered strength, becoming shriller and more insistent. He glanced back out of the window and saw that they were still as they were, save that the baboons seemed to be crouching to spring, rather than squatting, awaiting an order. And then he heard the woman's arm drop and swing lifeless over the side of the bed, and on that second, with one movement, they sprang, and Hoareb's scream was cut short in his throat.

When the Doctor uncovered his eyes and looked through the window again, the clearing was empty save for the leather whip, which lay where it had fallen.

As the Doctor looked, the little witch-doctor came from behind the mimosa trees and picked it up.

Then he advanced to below the window and raised his hand respectfully. "Perhaps the Master should return home," he suggested politely in Zulu. "There is little left for him to do here."

"I will," said the Doctor limply, and fainted flat on his face.

It was midnight by the time he had made his report to the police and reached his house, and his wife was still waiting supper. When she saw his face, however, she gave a wail of anxiety and hurried toward him.

"Jamie!" she cried. "Are you ill? Indeed you are! What shall I get you for it?"

He shook his head weakly.

"There's nothing I need, Agnes," he said with an unfamiliar meekness. "I've just seen a doctor."

Come Dance with Me on My Pony's Grave
by C. L. Grant

November, and an aged slate sky; a wind snapping across the fields like a bullwhip and cracking around a golden brown house that squatted warmly on the grey landscape.

Aaron, huddled in a winter-worn and crimson jacket, was slumped, seemingly relaxed, against the jamb of the open front door, his hands flat in his pockets. His eyes were narrowed against the wind, and they shifted quickly along the partially wooded horizon, blurring the Dakota spruce and pine to a green-and-grey smear of almost preternatural fear. Behind him the house was empty and silent. There was only the wind and an occasional wooden creak.

He shivered.

Suddenly an explosive gust caught him unprepared and shoved him off balance; a magazine was blown to the floor in the living room, and a shade snapped against glass. Reluctantly he closed the door and cut off the warmth from his back. His lips twisted into a half smile. A good thing Miriam's not here, he thought as his mind mimicked her laughing scold: Aaron Jackoson, what do you think we are—Eskimos? Just look at my curtains blown all over, and the cold, Aaron, the cold . . . He grinned, shook his head and closed his eyes briefly to allow her face to flash before him reassuringly. The wind gusted again, and his smile faded. Come home, Miriam, he thought (nearly prayed); come home soon—the boy frightens me yet.

Then he resettled himself to wait, arms folded and pressed tightly against his chest. He squinted into the cold, his eyes moving, moving as they had once been trained to do, watching and waiting . . .

. . . *under a multigreen canopy of broad leaves, twisted vines and knee-high, waist-high brush beside the paths he and his men rarely used as they climbed for hours through the bugs sweat heat dirt world. A ragged clearing ahead where the village so often visited was hidden, and the smoke-skinned, half-naked Montagnards who gave them the news that the enemy had long since fled—all save one, who, this time, belonged to them, not the soldiers. Water, then, with iodine tablets to kill the bacteria, and orange flavoring to kill the taste. While he watched the jungle and his men relaxed, finally. And the boy—eight, perhaps nine—stood by a black patch of earth where several men were racing the sun, digging what looked to be a grave. A shout . . .*

. . . and Aaron blinked and watched a slight figure break from the trees and zigzag swiftly across the field, arms waving wildly in greeting. He grinned and, pushing himself away from the house, limped heavily toward the fence as grass crackled sharply beneath his feet. He shivered and wondered how the boy had managed to adapt so rapidly to the four seasons so radically different from the hot and not-so-hot of the mountain jungles.

At last the boy reached the yard and with a melodramatic gasp draped himself over the faded white rail, his face darker, but not red, from exertion.

"Hey, dad."

"Hey, yourself."

"Boy, am I . . . bushed?"

Aaron nodded. "Bushed, pooped, beat, tired . . . in fact, you look like all of them rolled into one." He was tempted to ask where his adopted son had been, and thought better of it. "Come on inside, David, and get yourself warm. Your mother'll kill me if she finds I let you catch cold the minute she decides to go visiting."

The boy was thirteen and still quite short (would never be much taller), and as he dashed back to the house ahead of his father, his long straight black hair whipped his shoulders and the air, while Aaron watched carefully for hints of the past until he realized what he was doing and scolded himself silently for behaving like a damned fool. The boy, he insisted to his shadow, was an American now. But he could not help the growing feeling that, without Miriam, David thought of him only as the lieutenant who took him away. He glanced back at the trees and shut the door.

"Sit down, dad," David called from the kitchen. "I'll make you some hot tea. Did mother call today?"

"Yes, I'm afraid she already has," he answered. "About ten, ten-thirty. You were out with Pinto, I think."

"Nuts."

Aaron laughed and, after shucking his coat, stretched out on the sofa, letting the room draw the cold from his skin to die in the dark glow of the beams and paneled walls. And everywhere, the scent of Miriam.

Then he heard a cup shatter, and he sighed when David, none too quietly, began muttering to himself. "Hey, in there," he shouted. "We speak English in this house, remember?"

The boy poked his head out of the kitchen and grinned broadly. "Sorry, dad, but that's all I remember any more."

"The swearing?"

"But, dad, they're the best kind, don't you know? I heard the GIs use them all the time."

There was a sharp silence before David finally giggled and thrust out an open hand. "Look, dad, I was only counting. I don't remember any more than that, honest." He waited a moment, staring, then frowned and disappeared.

Now that's got to be a crime, Aaron thought, recalling all the tedious, impatient hours he had spent scraping together enough of the tribe's language to make himself, and his mission, understood; there were still a few isolated words and phrases that returned to him when he pressed, yet the boy had forgotten a lifetime. So he said. Once, when Aaron had been feeling particularly moody over his crippled leg, he had asked David if he minded being away from his old home, toppled through a sargasso of red tape and interviews into a country and life style as alien to the boy as the jungle was to Aaron. David had smiled, a little softly, and shaken his head. But the black eyes were expressionless; they always had been since the death of his father.

"Hey, dad! Quit daydreaming, please? This stuff is hot."

Aaron smiled and took the steaming cup from the offered tray. David sat cross-legged on the rug, watching intently as Aaron tasted the tea and nodded his approval. "Your mother," he said, "will be jealous."

David finally returned the smile, then turned his head toward the bay window as if he were plotting the darkening sky, listening for the invisible wind. He squirmed. Coughed. Aaron amused himself with the boy's impatience as long as he could; then, softly, "Pinto must be starving. Is he on a diet or something?"

And the boy was gone. To a pony named Pinto, horse enough for a youngster who would never be tall, not even average. They had both arrived on the same day, and five years later they were inseparable. Wild, Aaron thought. Both of them.

The telephone shrilled. Aaron grunted away a cramp that knifed his mine-shattered leg as he headed into the hallway and picked up the receiver.

"Jackoson, that you?"

Aaron winced. "Yes, Mr. Sorrentino, it's me."

"Damned good thing. Want to tell you those wolves are back again. Went after two of my rams this morning. Saw them. Big as horses they were. Chased them into the woods, I did." Right to my place, Aaron thought bitterly; thanks a lot. "I got a shot at them."

"You what?"

"Said I got a shot at them."

"Damn it, Sorrentino, my boy was playing there today. You know he always—"

"Did I hit him?" The voice was singularly unconcerned.

"Christ, no! If you had, do you think I'd be—"

"Then don't worry about it, Jackoson. I'm a perfect shot. I hit what I aim at. That kid—"

"My son."

"—won't get hurt, don't you worry about that. But one thing, Jackoson . . . I, uh, don't want to make any trouble, you understand, but I wish you would straighten out your kid about where your property ends. Him and that damn pony scare hell out of my sheep."

"If I didn't know you better, Mr. Sorrentino, I'd be tempted to think that you were somehow trying to threaten me."

A raucous laugh and a harsh gasping for breath. Aaron wanted to spit at the phone. "Just wanted you to know, Jackoson; don't get so worked up. You soldier boys get excited too easy."

"I just don't like the tone of your voice, Sorrentino."

"So sue me," Sorrentino said, and hung up.

Aaron breathed deeply and grabbed the edge of the hall table. "I could kill you so easily, Mr. Franklin Sorrentino," he said to the wall. "So goddamned easily."

"Dad?"

Aaron spun around to face the boy standing in the hall . . .

. . . standing by the gash of a grave while the jungle severed the sun's scattered light and a pit fire substituted shadows for trees. Lt. Jackoson shifted uneasily on the ground and lighted a cigarette as the boy stared at him. There was no recognition in the black bullet eyes, though the man and the boy had often played together whenever the squad came to stay and use the friendly village as a base. Now Jackoson saw only a new, weary emptiness, and deeper: a purpose. The grave was for the boy's father, the shaman of the tribe . . .

. . . the boy's voice was quiet. "I don't like him, dad." The words spun high, and Aaron shivered a remembrance while he stood in the tunnel-dark hall. David moved as silently as he spoke. Even on the Shetland he was noiseless—in the early days, when the boy was still learning, Miriam had said: he's like a ghost, Aaron, and he frightens me. In the early days. There were still remnants of the mountain in him, but Miriam no longer saw them. "He's greedy, dad, and doesn't . . . feel for things."

Aaron nodded, just barely stopping himself from patting the boy on the head. He had learned early that "sin" was too weak a word for such a gesture. Instead, he grabbed his shoulders. "Go watch some TV, son. Forget it. It's not worth worrying yourself."

They walked, the son just behind, into the living room and dimmed the lights. Before Aaron switched on the set, David curled into a corner chair where the age in his voice belied his thin body. "Why doesn't he like me, dad?"

Aaron knew this was not a time to smile away a question.

Five years before, his greatest fear had been what the other youngsters would think of his adopted son, but the smoke-grey skin and the hint of Polynesia in his features had given him instant acceptance, especially with the girls; David, however, was only superficially friendly always. "I don't know, son. Perhaps he's lonely with no children of his own, and that wife of his is enough for any man."

"He thinks I'm different." The tone said: he knows I'm different, and you're afraid that maybe he's right.

"Perhaps."

"I don't like him."

"David, he's not going to be the only one in your life to think you're . . . well, not the same as others. You're quite a unique young man."

"He hates Pinto. He say, last week when he run me away, it was a silly name for a horse. Pinto doesn't like him either. He try to kick his stomach once."

"Oh." Aaron, forgetting to correct the boy's English, thought he was beginning to understand Sorrentino's surliness.

"He missed."

In spite of himself, Aaron said, "Too bad."

The boy laughed quietly.

"Listen, David, Mr. Sorrentino doesn't really understand how you can . . . can *be* with animals. Most boys . . . do you know what rapport means?"

"No, dad, but I think I can make guesses."

"Well, good. Rapport, you see, isn't always explainable. Sometimes it's something that just happens or belongs to a way of life that people just can't grasp. Like . . ." and he stopped, thought, and decided not to mention the shaman. "And, if you don't mind my asking," he said instead, falsely lighter, "why did you name him Pinto?"

David laughed again. "It suits him."

"How? He's all brown?"

"It feels right, dad. It suits him. He runs and leaps and . . . he's like me in many ways. His name is right."

"Well, Sorrentino can't understand that, son."

"I know. He doesn't . . . feel. I don't like him."

Aaron frowned in concentration, seeking the words that would stifle the hatred he knew the boy was feeling. It was wrong to allow this to fester, wrong not to show the boy that some men must be tolerated, that, as the saying goes, it takes all kinds. He tried, but he took too long.

"I'm going to bed, dad. Good night." David uncurled from the chair, stayed out of the light until his bedroom door closed behind him. Always closed. Sanctum.

Aaron hesitated in following, then sat again. For the first time since they had been together, David had lied to him. So blatantly, in fact, that its very obviousness pained more than the deceit itself. The language. He knew David had not forgotten all but the numbers. Once in a while, from behind the door, a muttering filtered through the house and filled him with dreams. Songs chanted on horseback across the fields and through the half-light in the pines; the whisperings to the animals. Black hair and black eyes and a strength in slender arms that contradicted their frailty. Montagnard. Mountain dweller. Outcast.

Christ! he thought, and chided himself for allowing his mind to become so morbid. The weather, his leg and Miriam's absence were getting to be too much. He decided to call her first thing in the morning and ask her to cut her visit short. Her mother wasn't that lonely, and he needed her laughter.

He dozed fitfully until the telephone twisted him stiffly from the couch. His watch had stopped. He stood, scratching his head vigorously, then stretched his arms over his head. "All right," he mumbled. "All right, all right, for god's sake." *Daylight,* he thought in amazement. That little dope didn't even wake me so I could sleep in a bed; how the hell did I oversleep? Glancing at the front window, he noticed streaks on the glass and the shimmer of ice on the walk. Rain, freezing rain was the last thing he needed, with David pouting and his wife gone. For a moment he was ready to let the phone ring and crawl into bed to hide. The house and that damned phone were making him nervous.

Still rubbing the sleep from his face, he leaned awkwardly against the wall and snatched up the receiver. "Yeah, yeah, Jackoson here."

"Aaron, this here is Will."

He stiffened. "Yes, sheriff, what can I do for you?" There were excited noises in the background; a man was bellowing angrily.

"I'm over at the Sorrentino place. You'd better get over here."

"David?"

"No, nothing's happened to the boy. But Sorrentino accidentally shot the pony. He's dead."

"I'll be right there." No thought, then; only an endless stream of cursing accusations: half in relief for his son's safety, half in anger at the rancher's murder of the boy's pet. His coat, first jamming on its hanger, refused to slide on easily. The pickup stalled twice. He shook uncontrollably, and his leg throbbed.

The truck skidded on the icy road, but Aaron, barely aware that he was driving at all, ignored the warning. Twice in two days he had wanted to kill, and twice he was unashamed for it.

There were two town patrol cars parked on the shoulder of the road when he arrived, and he nearly ran up the back of one as he slid to a halt and scrambled out. There was a small crowd hunched coldly in the vast, well-tended yard: police, several neighbors looking ill at ease, Sorrentino himself pounding his arms against the air by the sheriff, and David standing quietly to one side . . .

. . . while the oldest men carefully lowered the body of the shaman into the oversized grave. They scuttled away, then, and the boy stepped up to drop in the trappings of his father's profession, a lock of his own hair, a brown seed, a young branch freshly cut. They buried the war-murdered man beneath black earth and passed the remainder of the night mourning. Lt. Jackoson continued to watch the boy—a one-time, now distant friend. He watched the boy sitting calmly on the grave, staring at the prisoner, a scarred man in a tattered blue uniform. Jackoson had warned his men to mind their own business this time, and they did, gratefully; but few slept and all were uneasy. And still the little boy stared . . .

. . . at the ground until Aaron placed an arm lightly around his shoulders and he looked up. No greeting. A look was all. Sheriff Jenkins, a scowl and sympathy fighting in his face, walked hurriedly over, with Sorrentino directly behind him. Aaron glared at them, barely able to contain the rage he felt for his son. "How?" he demanded without preliminaries. Sorrentino tried to bull forward, but Jenkins held up a hand to stop him.

"Frank here called me about forty-five minutes ago, Aaron. Said he was afraid he'd shot your son."

"I was just inside the wood, Jackoson," Sorrentino said, his voice oddly harsh. "I was chasing them wolves. I heard this noise right where I spotted them last, so I let go—"

"Without being sure?" Momentarily, Aaron was too appalled at the big man's stupidity to be angry. "You know kids are playing in there all the time. My God, Frank, you're a good enough shot to have waited a . . ." He stopped, seeing the retreat in the other man's eyes. "You . . ." He shook his head to clear it. "You . . . no, you couldn't have. Not even you."

"Now wait a damn minute, Jackoson."

"Shut up a minute, Frank."

"But, sheriff, that man just accused me of deliberately killing that kid's animal!"

"He didn't say that, did he?"

Sorrentino sputtered, then wheeled and stalked away, muttering. Jenkins didn't watch him leave; Aaron did. "Listen, Aaron, I couldn't find any evidence that it happened any other way than he said. I know how you two feel about each other, but as far as I'm concerned, his story holds up. I'm sorry, Aaron, but it was an accident."

Aaron nodded, though he was just as sure the sheriff was wrong.

"Look, if you want, the boys and I will take the—"

"No," David said.

Aaron saw the look on Jenkins' face and knew it was the first thing David had said that morning. Against his better judgment he agreed. "We'll take him, Will. But thanks anyway. I'd appreciate it if some of your men would help me put him in the truck."

The sheriff started to say something, but the boy walked between them, past the neighbors to the truck, where he let down the gate and stood by, waiting.

"The boy wasn't on the pony," Will said. "It must have wandered off while Davie was playing."

Aaron nodded. And what, he thought, was David playing?

Pinto's head had been hastily wrapped in a blanket now matted with blood. David sat stroking the animal's rigid flank. Through the rear-view mirror, Aaron could see the hand moving smoothly over the cooling flesh. In his own eyes were the stirrings of tears. For once he thought he knew how the boy felt, to lose a friend, much more than a pet. He drove slowly, turning off the road just before his own land began. There was a rutted path leading into the wood to a clearing where the boys of the surrounding farms had erected forts and castles, trenches and space ships. At its western end was a slight rise, and it was there that they sweated in the cold noon of the grey slate day and buried Pinto. The wind was listless; the rain had stopped. When the grave was filled, Aaron walked painfully back to the truck to wait for David, and an hour passed before they were headed for home, and all the way Aaron tried vainly to joke the boy back into a fair humor, even promising him a new pet as soon as they could get into town. David, however, only stared at the road, one hand unconsciously working at his throat.

Immediately they arrived at the house, the telephone rang and Aaron grabbed for it, hoping it was Miriam. It was Sorrentino, apologizing and sounding unsettlingly desperate; and Aaron, eager to talk, eager to turn from his son's depression, profusely acknowledged the other's story, and damned himself as he spoke. Sorrentino kept on. And on. He was babbling, Aaron realized, very often incoherent, and in his puzzlement at the rancher's behavior, he responded in kind, knowing he sounded like an idiot, trying not to admit that he was somehow, inexplicably afraid of his own son.

When Sorrentino at last rang off, Aaron felt rather than saw the boy's bedroom door open. He would not turn. He was not going to watch grief harden the young face. "It'll be all right, son," he said weakly. "In time. In time. You . . . you have to give it time."

The boy was a shadow. "He could see, dad."

"We can't prove that, son."

"He could see everything. The brush isn't that high."

"David, we cannot prove it. Things are different here; you know that. We have to prove things first."

And still he did not turn.

"He did it on purpose. You know that, and you won't do anything. You know it and . . ."

Turn around, you old fool. He's only a boy. He's only a boy, for God's sake . . .

. . . for God's sake, the lieutenant thought as he watched the boy sitting on the grave, how long is he going to stay there? His eyes, burning from the darkness and the fire's acrid smoke, shifted to the prisoner. The man was staring at the shaman's son, entranced, it seemed, and unmoving. He was unbound, but none of the tribesmen seemed to care. They were confident with knowledge that Jackoson didn't have, and Jackoson didn't like it. He tried instead to think of home and a place where people behaved the way they were supposed to . . .

. . . behave yourself, stupid, he thought, and send the boy to bed. He'll feel better in the morning.

"You'd better lie down now, dad," the shadow said. "Your leg must be hurting after all that digging."

Aaron closed his eyes and nodded, feeling for the first time since leaving the house eons ago the painful strain that nearly buckled him. A moment later he felt the boy's arm around his waist, guiding him firmly to the bedroom. In the dim curtained light, he watched David prepare the bed, then stand aside while he eased himself between the cold sheets. David smiled at him.

"We'll . . . we'll see the sheriff again in a few days, son. We'll talk to him."

"Sure, dad."

"And David, don't . . . I mean, you know, don't try to do anything on your own—you know what I mean? I mean, don't go off chasing his sheep into the next county or smashing windows. Okay?"

The boy paused in the doorway. "Sure, dad. You want your medicine?"

"No, thanks. I'll be all right in a little while. Just call me for dinner."

"Okay. I'm going to read or something. You need anything, please call."

Aaron smiled. "Go on, son." And after the door closed, he wondered, not for the first time, if he had been right in taking the boy away. Neither, in half a decade, seemed closer to understanding the other than when they had started out on the plane from Saigon. They spoke the same language, shared the same house, but the rapport David had with the animals, with Pinto, was missing between father and son. The war was no longer a threat; its use as a bond had dissolved.

I don't know my own son, he thought.

A part of his mind told him to stop feeling sorry for himself: the problem wasn't a new one.

I'm not feeling sorry for myself.

You sound like one of Miriam's soap operas.

I don't.

He's an ordinary boy who needs time. He's seen war.

He's had five years, and so, by the way, have I.

And when he slept, he dreamt of a slight mound in a path supposedly cleared and the sound he felt and heard before waking screaming in a hospital in Japan with a leg raw and twisted. He had refused amputation. He needed the leg.

When he opened his eyes, it was dark. He tried to fall asleep again, but a rising wind nudged him back to wakefulness. Finally he swung out of bed and dressed quietly. He was hungry and thirsty. Cautiously, he crept into the kitchen to fix a snack and unaccountably remembered a rancher he knew in passing who had a string of Shetlands he rented to pony rides during the summer fairs. Maybe, he thought, he could persuade this man to part with one of his animals on credit. It would be easy enough to explain what had happened to Pinto. The man would have to help him. Slowly the idea grew, hurrying his actions, making him grin at himself. Without stopping to drink the coffee he had poured, he hastened down the hall to David's room.

It was empty. His boots were gone, and his jacket. There

was a hint of panic before Aaron realized that David, still mourning, had probably gone out to the barn to Pinto's stall. Snatching his coat from the closet, he rushed outside, gasping once at the cold air and the strong wind that slid across the now-frozen ground. A digging pain in his thigh caused him to slow down, but long before he'd flung open the barn door, he knew the building would be empty. He stood in the barnyard, aimlessly turning, seeking a direction to travel, until he saw the faint orange glow over the trees. He stared, hands limp at his sides, squinting, thinking, denying all the fears that founded his nightmares. He knew his century and still refused to believe what he had seen on the jungled mountain, dreaded what he might see if he followed the light.

It was just before dawn . . .

. . . *and Lt. Jackoson was the only squad member still awake, the others sleeping in luxurious safety for the first time in days. Night noises. Night wind. He was drowsy and rubbed the blur from his eyes. Curiosity prodded him; he rubbed his eyes again. The fire burned sullenly at the side of the grave. The boy was naked, now, and standing . . .*

. . . running over the ice-crusted ground, Aaron was pushed from behind by the wind. He ignored his leg as long as he could, concentrating on the wavering line of trees ahead. Then, just inside the tiny wood, his foot pushed through a hidden burrow and he slammed to the ground. Palms, knees, forehead stung. When he tried to stand, his leg wrenched out from under him, and he cried out. Before him, trunks and branches, brush and grass twisted slowly in the light of the fire, weaving darkness within darkness. Aaron pushed himself to one leg, his teeth clamped to his lips and, using the trees for support, hobbled toward the clearing. His left leg went numb, the pain felt only from the hip, and finally he collapsed.

Not now, he begged, not now!

He crawled, forearms and one foot, seeing his breath puff in front of his face, seeing his hands turn a dry red from the cold. Then there was a break in the pine, and he saw the boy . . .

. . . *on his father's grave, shuffling slowly from side to side, humming to himself as he stared at the mound beneath his feet. The tribe had reassembled, squatting in the shadows, silent. The pit fire cracked . . .*

. . . on the rise, and the smell of burning pine pierced the brittle air. And between himself and his son, Aaron saw . . .

. . . *the prisoner seemingly rooted in place, turned so his face was hidden. The boy, not looking up, not acknowledging the world's existence, muttered something and the man shuddered . . .*

. . . beneath his heavy, fur-trimmed hunting jacket. There was a rifle, useless now, dangling from one hand. Aaron tried to push himself up, to stand, but the agony was too great, and at the moment all he wanted was the heat from the fire that silhouetted the boy . . .

. . . *shuffling faster, mumbling in rapid bursts while the prisoner swayed, slipped back, then lurched forward. Slowly, toward the grave, in the light of the fire. Jackoson thought he was dreaming . . .*

. . . but the cold was too real, and he wondered how the boy, so lately his son, could stand the wind that whipped the flames from side to side and drew . . .

. . . *the prisoner toward them, stiff-jointed like a grotesque marionette. The jungle . . .*

. . . the clearing was quiet, and Aaron could hear the boy, chanting now, urging, taunting the big man forward. Aaron tried shouting, but his throat was too dry, his mind unable to break loose his tongue. All he could see was the rifle glinting. Sorrentino moved. Lumbered. Silent.

Prisoner/rancher reached the grave.

The boy, still chanting, reached out, palms up, waiting until the other grasped them (the rifle dropping soundlessly). A pair now, circling in slow motion. Dirt shifted beneath their feet. Aaron watched . . .

. . . *more drowsy still from the fire's heat and the boy's monotonic voice, still undecided whether or not he was dreaming . . .*

. . . numb from the cold and drawing blood from his lips as he fought the pain enshrouding his thoughts. He lay flat on the ground, his head barely raised, his eyes glazed.

The boy abruptly dropped his hands and stepped down from the grave.

The prisoner waited, standing, and made no attempt to resist when the shaman's hand/pony's teeth reached through the earth and took hold.

Jackoson slept, thought he was dreaming.

Aaron fainted, thought he was screaming.

David, smiling, picked up a shovel.